HEATHER BOYD

Hardly a Stranger

HUNT CLUB – 3

The characters and events portrayed in this book are fictitious.
Any similarity to real persons, living or dead, is purely coincidental
and not intended by the author.

HARDLY A STRANGER
Copyright © 2011 by Heather Boyd
Edited by Sandra Sookoo

All rights reserved. No part of this book may be reproduced in any
form by any electronic or mechanical means—except in the case of
brief quotations embodied in critical articles or reviews—without
written permission.

For more information visit: www.heather-boyd.com

DEDICATION

My love and gratitude to my family for understanding
my obsession and being interested in what I do.

By Heather Boyd

Almost an Equal
Barely a Master
Hardly a Stranger

Just a Dream
Never a Gentleman
Once a Husband

CHAPTER ONE

Too young. Too old. Too forward. Balding, fat, stupid and bilious. Was there no one in London whose company deserved the attention of an unattached man? Ambrose Manning, Duke of Staines, scanned the gentlemen seated closest to him in his exclusive club—his pride and joy for the last decade—with growing annoyance. Not one of them attracted him physically or mentally and he desperately wanted some form of pleasure today. Why the hell had he issued invitations to so many unappealing lords? He surely hadn't invited them for their deep pockets and large appetites for the finer things in life.

When he'd first conceived of the Hunt Club, he'd wanted a place where like-minded individuals, well-connected lords and deep-pocketed gentlemen, could be comfortable and indulge their many and varied appetites in absolute privacy. Yet none of those seated around him, men of vice and excess, seemed to whet his.

A definite problem and one he was having a great deal of trouble accepting as he aged. He would turn five and forty next month. Was this to be the best life could offer?

He hoped to hell it wasn't, otherwise he might go shrieking mad with frustration and develop blue balls. He was not looking forward to his next birthday celebration. Ambrose heaved a sigh at the thought of that approaching milestone. There were days when he felt as ancient as the gnarled oaks lining the riverbanks at Tindel Park, his ancestral home.

As he drew the memory of his distant estate deep into his being, Mr. Robert Banks, the Duke of Lewes' young heir, threaded his way through the club's many patrons. Ambrose sighed with relief at the distraction from his maudlin thoughts as Banks stopped nearby.

"May I join you, Your Grace?"

He smiled in encouragement. "Of course, Mr. Banks. Do join me. Would you care for a brandy?"

"Thank you."

Ambrose signaled a footman to bring the youth a snifter and regarded the serious man. The Duke of Lewes had asked him to keep a close eye on his nephew while he cavorted on the Continent with his lover. Given that Banks was fresh up to Town, and very, very naïve, he had readily agreed to take him under his wing while he found his feet in society.

As a favor to Lewes, Banks had been invited to the club several months ago now, and seemed content enough about it. But he had not discovered the full range of services offered to patrons so far. To date, he'd only partaken of the same courtesan each time he ventured upstairs. The lovely Felicity had more than one gentleman dangling after her. Not Ambrose, of course. He never dabbled with his employees, but his own restrictions meant, quite exasperatingly, that he had to find his pleasure among the gentlemen and ladies he met in society. By no means an easy task. A man like Banks attracted a much larger crowd of admirers than an older man of nearly five and forty.

When Banks fidgeted for the third time under his scrutiny, Ambrose leaned toward Banks. "Is anything amiss?"

A guilty flush swept over his cheeks. "Am I that obvious?"

Ambrose smiled to reduce the sting. "You are honest, sir. There is nothing to worry about in that. Given enough time you'll be able to mask your emotions as well as the rest of us."

Mr. Banks nodded. "It's about my mother."

Ambrose wasn't surprised. "What has the delightful Mrs. Banks done now?"

"She's taken up with Singleton." Banks scowled fiercely. "I don't care for the chap sniffing 'round her skirts."

He pursed his lips. "Singleton is a fine man, no scandal or hint of stain to his reputation. What has he done to offend you?"

"It is not what he's done, but what my mother has. She sings."

Lewes had mentioned the boy's tendency to pout, but Ambrose still frowned at the outburst. "I take it she cannot carry a tune?"

"My mother sings well enough. It's the subject matter that vexes me. She sings of frolicking and newborn sons for heaven's sake."

Ambrose snorted. "She sounds like a woman in love."

"How can you tell?" Banks leaned forward. "This Singleton seems like a decent chap on the surface, but he must be very poorly connected if you have not invited him here."

Singleton was entirely too straight-laced for the club. He'd tell the world what went on here behind closed doors and Ambrose couldn't allow that. "You are correct that Singleton is not a member, nor would he ever receive an invitation. The club is not for every man. But Banks, people in love do the strangest things. They sing, they smile, they might even leave the country. But falling in love isn't a bad experience."

"Were you ever in love?"

Pain tightened his chest. "I loved my wife, very much."

"Yes, but . . . you've never fallen into that trap again."

"Not so far. Listen, Banks, I know your parents were hardly a love match and you undoubtedly have good reasons for your opinions, but love does not render one weak. It gives strength, too. I am envious of friends who have found love."

Very envious. He shifted uncomfortably. Two of his friends had found love recently and were blissfully happy with the outcome. Byworth had his Henry tucked away in the country, Lewes had run off with his Terrance to the Continent, leaving Ambrose to wonder what was wrong with him that he was still alone after fifteen years a widow. Did a man only love strongly once in his lifetime?

His wife, Anna, God rest her soul, had been the perfect woman: captivating in public, utterly priceless at home. He had doted on her so much that when she'd died suddenly after a mere ten years of marriage his heart had shattered into a thousand pieces—pieces that had taken many years to re-form. But perhaps he had never mended at all. Perhaps he was destined to live forever lonely.

"Well, I shan't ever fall for that poppycock."

Ah, to be young again and so stupidly ignorant. Love, in all its wondrous forms, was what made life worth living. Even the love of family and friends soothed the soul. He may never find that perfect peace again as he had with Anna, but he still hoped to come close. He leaned toward Banks and companionably slapped his shoulder. "I would suggest you do not make such startling pronouncements because if one day you should fall in love I shall tease you mercilessly upon the discovery." He softened his words with a smile.

Taking on Banks' education while his uncle was from the country was no great hardship, and he would have some truly wonderful things to tease the young man about later in his life if he did not learn to moderate his startling outbursts.

Banks' demeanor turned sullen. "So, about Singleton?"

Ambrose laughed. "Rest easy. He could be good for your mother. Just think, if she has truly formed a *tendré* for him he will keep her occupied and out of your affairs."

The boy smiled suddenly. "I never thought of that. I say, that could be very good."

He quirked an eyebrow. "Do not get too carried away. She still has eyes in the back of her head." And if she had discovered her brother-in-law's preference for other men and accepted it without a qualm then there was no secret she couldn't overturn. "Never underestimate a mother."

"I won't."

Ambrose smiled fondly when Banks took his leave to join a younger group of men across the room, but an odd ache burned in his chest that perhaps Banks didn't belong here either. He was an amiable man, if prone to sulks, handsome and neat in his habits. He would make a fine duke one day, hopefully after the current Duke of

Lewes had lived a long and happier life with his lover, Terrance. As far as Ambrose could tell, Banks knew nothing about that.

"He's pretty," a high-pitched male voice muttered behind his back where Redding should have stood if he were not otherwise engaged.

He turned and found Lord Silas Flint, last season's late inductee to the club, scowling after Mr. Banks like a jealous lover. He'd better not let the man get the wrong ideas about Banks' nature. Not every man admitted to the club dabbled in trousers. And those who didn't ignored those who did unless they wished to be expelled and vice versa. He wanted no trouble or misunderstanding among the patrons. The club was for pleasure only. "The Duke of Lewes' heir recently joined our merry band."

"Ah." Lord Silas slid into the chair Banks had occupied. "An untouchable then. You must be disappointed he is out of bounds."

The idea of a liaison with young Banks was revolting. The boy was his friend's family and certainly not his type. Ambrose wished Redding was here to scowl at Lord Silas. His footman was very good at dissuading others from overstepping where they were not wanted. Ambrose had regretted inviting Lord Silas after one short week of membership because the man seemed to think that Ambrose was interested in him personally.

He forced a smile to his lips and ignored Lord Silas' suggestion. "You're back in London again. Did you enjoy Fletcherly's house party?"

Lord Silas crossed his legs, nudging Ambrose in the process. "Utterly boring event. I was fooled into believing half the *ton* would be in attendance. Can't think of why Fletcherly married that cow-faced hag."

For the money, of course. Fletcherly had been up to his eyebrows in debt before he married. Once he had her funds, he'd resumed extravagant life and week-long house parties were a common event.

Lord Silas scanned the room around them. He smiled suddenly. "But enough of him. Are you engaged for the evening? I thought perhaps we might dine together." He batted his lashes and Ambrose almost laughed as the action caused the opposite effect Lord Silas wished for.

When Ambrose wanted a woman, he bedded a woman. But when he bedded a man, he did not want fluttering lashes or simpering. There was no greater cure for lust than a man who tended to foppishness. He liked strong men, confident men.

He sighed heavily with feigned regret. "I have plans for the evening."

Lord Silas smiled. "Perhaps we are invited to the same entertainment. I should be available to you at any time." While he spoke, he stroked his own arm. Ambrose ignored the signal that everyone in his club learned to recognize as a clandestine invitation for dalliance. Usually, the signal was reserved for the footmen, male whores hidden in plain sight. Ambrose wasn't too keen Lord Silas made the gesture to him where anyone in the club could see.

He stood and tugged on his waistcoat. "Another time, Lord Silas. Now, if you will excuse me, I have some club business to attend to."

Ambrose quickly left the public rooms behind with relief. Despite his interest in bedding men on occasion, it had to be the right man. Lord Silas wouldn't be his choice tonight or any night, but he did need someone and soon to take the edge off his appetite for the forbidden before he did something utterly foolish.

CHAPTER TWO

A man should do his best work at all times or he'd never respect himself. The ethics of hard work and loyalty was what Francis Redding's poor farmer father had drilled into him and his brother every day until he died. Albus Redding had been the proudest father when his youngest son had taken up duties at Tindel Park, the Duke of Staines' country estate. Francis doubted he would be pleased that he'd become a surgeon to a brothel full of whores at the current duke's request.

Not that he'd had a chance to be surgeon for anyone else. As a farmer's son, Francis lacked the formal education to become more than a layman at the task. But he did apply himself as best he could so the duke would never regret his impulsive suggestion that he learn the surgeon's trade when he'd revealed his curiosity. Outside of farming, Francis was the only Redding to have made something of himself beyond harvesting hay.

He carefully pulled the stitch tight and gently tied it off. Even so, the whore he worked on whimpered in pain. He studied the damaged quim before him and wiped a smear of blood from her skin. "Almost done, Felicity."

"I know, sir." She sniffled, but Francis could understand her worry. The girl had had a rough night and been damaged by Lord Carter's unnecessary enthusiasm. He'd ripped her as if she'd been a virgin, not the experienced courtesan she was reputed to be. The duke would have to do something about Carter. This was the third girl in as many weeks requiring some form of attention who Francis had worked on.

When he was satisfied the stitching was his best work, he cleared his instruments away, drew Felicity's nightgown over her knees and tucked the sheets close around her. He met her gaze. "No customers for you for a while. You'll need time to heal. I'll be back tomorrow to check on your progress."

"Mrs. Marinari won't like that."

"Don't worry about that vixen. I'll deal with her directly."

Even sore and battered as she was, Felicity offered him a coy smile. "Thank you, Mr. Redding. When I'm well again you can have me for free. I'm ever so keen to repay your kindness today."

He smiled at the offer, but they both knew he would decline. "Just rest there for as long as you can each day."

A good surgeon did not bed his customers in exchange for payment, no matter the trade they worked in. The whores at the Hunt Club trusted him to heal their hurts, not molest them when he had them laid out before him. But in all honesty, the sights afforded by a whore's spread legs rarely produced an excited rise. Perhaps it was because their favors were given so freely that he did not trust one word of flirting encouragement that came out of their mouths. It was not their fault—they were paid to sound encouraging. And the Duke of Staines, their employer, would fire any of them if they said what was really on their minds.

Francis would have to speak up about Lord Carter's rough ways with the whores. The loss of Felicity, along with the other two, from the roster for the next week would cost the duke quite a sum of money. Staines did not like to waste anything in his club and would no doubt become annoyed.

Wearily, he returned to his private chamber where he stored his daily needs at the club and tugged on the bell for assistance. Cook would send up hot water for washing now that he was finished with Felicity and then he would resume his post as footman, six paces behind the Duke of Staines. A position he'd held since he was a wide eyed boy of ten among the ducal finery.

These days, he didn't notice the splendor so much. Strange to think he'd grown so accustomed to the Duke of Staines and his many possessions that he felt a certain pride in the estate. A misplaced sense of ownership he should disabuse himself of as soon as the warm sensations began. Yet Tindel Park and the London townhouse *were* home. He'd lived within those walls for more than thirty years.

Francis methodically unwrapped the bundle of instruments from the bloodied cloth and laid them in the basin for cleaning. The sharp edge of the scissors caught a speck of sunlight from the world outside and their ghastly appearance sent a chill of unease down his spine.

He jumped as someone bumped against the door. "Come."

A maid rushed in carrying a kettle of hot water and then rushed out again without looking at him with more than a bare glance. Puzzled, he looked down. No wonder. A dark stain of blood marred his pale grey silk waistcoat. The sight of a surgeon smeared with blood would cause anyone nightmares. He must have had some on his hand and accidentally transferred it to the expensive cloth.

Francis ripped his soiled waistcoat off and discovered the blood had seeped through to his newest white shirt, too. Damn the blood. He removed his cravat and shirt too then poured half of the near-boiling water over his instruments and the rest in the washbasin, along with some cold so he did not scald himself.

He sank his hands into the basin, watching the remnants of his surgery mingle with the fresh water. He shuddered. Perhaps it was time to find a new profession. If not for the duke's need for a discreet surgeon at the club, he would never have begun the trade in the first place. He was heartily sick of the trade and thought longingly of his fantasy of becoming a physician, a position that did not require one to dabble in blood but merely dispense advice from a distance.

He grabbed a washcloth and scrubbed his hands clean, washed his face free of sweat and then wiped at the blood smear on his belly. He had little chance of becoming a physician, even if he did study the lore in every available moment. The role required greater consequence and attendance at a university such as Cambridge.

"Now that is a sight worth getting aroused for. Good

God, the duke could charge double to have a man like you join our ranks," a feminine voice purred.

Francis didn't turn around as the Hunt Club's abbess invaded his chamber. "Not all of the duke's servants are destined to be whores, Marinari."

Marinari managed everything about the girls except their health. She clothed, styled and allocated them for the patron's pleasure. She could also be a pain in the arse for everyone else in between.

"I cannot see why not." She flounced into the room with a loud rustle of fabric and perched on his only chair, her pretty face twisted with distaste. "It's far preferable to stitching them up."

He sighed and waggled a finger at her. "If I turned whore for the duke who would clean up your customers' mistakes?"

Her smile turned grim. "That man should have his balls removed for his wickedness," her voice came out as a low pitched growl, reminding Francis that he was actually dealing with a man beneath all that dazzling beauty. There were days when he tended to forget. Or maybe he merely wanted to ignore that some men liked to dress in fine silks and lace and parade about as women. Mrs. Angela Marinari was really Mr. Angelo Marinari, previously of Italy and with no other socially acceptable profession he could speak of.

"Who is to lose their bollocks?" the Duke of Staines asked from the open doorway, his face set in angry lines.

Mrs. Marinari started at the interruption, but then smiled sweetly in the blink of an eye. "Oh, no one, Your Grace." She curtsied and hurried out.

Staines closed the door behind him and leaned against it. His chest swelled as he drew in a large breath then let it out slowly. "I was wondering where you'd got to until I heard your skills were required this morning."

The strain of the morning closed about Francis and he set his hand to the back of the chair for balance. "Lord Carter, again. You must do something about him this time."

Staines crossed the room and stopped within inches, a

frown marring his usually happy expression. "I must?"

Francis nodded. "Yes, Your Grace. I had to stitch Miss Felicity's nether region today."

The duke winced.

Acid curled in Francis' belly at the memory. He set a hand on his stomach as emotion rolled through him. "Yes, again. It is not her fault. He is far too rough with her and the others."

Staines mirrored his action and set a hand to his stomach, too. "Last time, he claimed he was enraptured by the new girl."

Francis shook his head at the duke's stubbornness not to see the truth. "Three times is no accident. The earl is little better than a rutting animal."

Carter plowed with little care for the whore beneath him and no consideration for her pleasure either. Men like that had once disgusted Staines. Had the duke ceased to notice and care?

Staines regarded him, his lips quirking upward. "Why are you the only one who will argue with me?"

He slumped to a chair wearily and rubbed his hands over his face. "Because it amuses you to let me, Your Grace."

Staines nodded, his gaze softened. "You look dead on your feet. Which reminds me, today is your day off. You should not be here."

"I had—"

The duke waved his hands to silence him. "Yes, yes, you had a woman in need of your skills and we are very grateful, but you've done your best. Go enjoy what's left of your day."

Francis regarded the duke warily. Even though he'd been gifted with an additional day off from his duties each month as a reward for faithful service, he was loath to take them. His family worked from sunup 'till sundown and the only time they left the farm was to attend church. When he compared his day with that of his brother, he lived a spoiled and pampered life. A life of further idleness, without responsibilities, sat ill with him. And since the duke was prone to accidents of all descriptions, and misunderstandings frequently occurred when Francis wasn't around, he hadn't been overly concerned to lose the day off.

The duke stuck out his left hand. "Come on, get up and out of this mad house before I change my mind and force you to attend Fairmont's ball with me. Lady Fairmont let slip that her companion was quite keen on you."

He shuddered at the thought and the duke laughed at him.

"In that case, I'll see you tomorrow morning at six, as usual."

Francis groaned. Six was such an ungodly hour for riding about in Hyde Park. Yet the duke insisted upon the exercise and so they rode together in relative privacy. Every other sensible lord was abed at that hour.

He placed his right hand in the duke's left and was hauled to his feet. Eye to eye, the duke was an imposing man. Handsome, determined, and with a playful streak a mile wide. At least Staines didn't dump him on his arse today as he had several days ago.

The grip on his hand slackened and slid up his arm.

As always, the tight ropes of desire spun upward from that brief caress. Francis' pulse hammered as the duke licked his lips. But then His Grace took a step back and about-faced. He waved as he hurried for the door. "Till the morning, Red. Try to have fun without me."

Francis shook his head. The duke baffled him, even after thirty-odd years in his service. He doubted he would ever work out what that man wanted from one minute to the next. They were hardly equals, but far more than strangers. The duke frequently sought him out for company when he was bored, drunk or wanted to discuss a vexing matter. That wasn't how most noblemen acted around their personal servants. Whatever the reason, Francis didn't mind too much. The duke had a wicked sense of humor.

Yet there were moments between them when he almost couldn't breathe when he sensed the duke was thinking of doing sinful things in his company, but, inevitably, Staines always drew back. Perhaps he forgot, momentarily, that Francis was a farmer's son.

Resigned to the inevitable day off, Francis cleaned his tools, redressed swiftly and left his chamber and the club. But rather than appropriate the duke's carriage, as he was allowed to do, he enjoyed a quiet walk home toward Golden Square, albeit via a circular route through Bond Street. He stopped at Gilbert and Hamilton Booksellers of London to see if his latest order had arrived.

"You've got the devil's luck, Mr. Redding."

Francis grinned as he tucked his hat under his arm. "Is that so, Mr. Gilbert? I take it my book has been found."

"Indeed it has, sir. Just in this very morning and I have something that might interest you more. *Observations on Medical Electricity* and some others. Can I interest you in taking a look?"

Redding set his hat on the counter. "I am yours to amaze and bedazzle."

Mr. Gilbert grinned and shuffled off, wincing as he went. "They're still in the backroom. Come see."

"What happened to your limb, Mr. Gilbert?"

"Oh, just carelessness. A scratch."

He frowned at what had to be a very painful injury. "A scratch that produces such a great limp should not be ignored. Better let me look at you first before I attend to the books. Sit down and show me where it hurts."

The older man slowly lifted is trouser leg. "You're not going to chop my limb off, are you?"

Francis smiled at the common question. "I've rarely been required to. This is infected, though. See the red at the edges? It needs proper attention. Can Mr. Hamilton handle the shop awhile?"

So, instead of spending the afternoon quietly studying to be a physician, he used his surgeon's skills to attend Mr. Gilbert's limb, then set off for the duke's residence with his arms full of medical books as night fell. In gratitude, and in lieu of payment, Gilbert had reduced the price of the books considerably. He had enough to read for the next two weeks, if the duke's social engagements were low. Four, if the duke was restless and attended frequent society affairs. Unfortunately, the former wasn't likely.

Francis slipped up the back stairs of Tindel House with a nod to the housekeeper and locked himself in his chamber for the night. He wouldn't be disturbed, aside from the housekeeper sending up a dinner tray when she had a moment to spare. He had endless hours of reading before him, he just had to choose which book would be the most beneficial to his future and would keep his mind from imagining the mischief the duke could get into overnight at Lord Fairmont's ball.

CHAPTER THREE

Ambrose had flirted with three widows, two men and still had not found the right lover for the evening. All he could think about was the wide expanse of Redding's abdomen, damp with water from his wash and the thin line of hair that disappeared beneath the band of his trousers. He groaned as he kissed the air above Lady Russell's hand after their dance and took his leave of her. She'd been more than willing. Experienced, adventurous and she *was* possessed of a large pair of breasts. Of course Redding, having accidentally stumbled upon her entertaining a lover, had once referred to them as overripe turnips and Ambrose had been hard pressed to hold in his mirth whenever he'd glanced down while they danced tonight.

He almost turned to his servant, but then remembered belatedly that he'd sent the man away for the night. Annoyed to have almost spoken into empty air, he threaded his way through Fairmont's ballroom until he reached a quieter area of the card room. Little groups clustered around the tables to watch the play underway. For a moment he did consider joining them, but he was too restless to sit still for cards and uninterested in losing his money. Redding claimed he should just toss coins over his shoulder for the poor to take as he strolled along instead of pretending to understand the first thing about winning at cards.

Perhaps Redding was right. Perhaps Ambrose had no luck but what could be spared on infrequent evenings. And tonight did not seem to be his lucky night, so far. He was bored out of his mind and frustrated as hell. He couldn't even approach Fairmont now. His former lover had taken to marriage and his young bride with startling single-mindedness and had turned aside all suggestions for further rendezvous.

Marriage to the right woman could do that. It could make a debauched rake something of a lapdog. Ambrose had been the very same when his own wife had been alive and didn't resent Fairmont's defection to the fairer sex. Lady Fairmont was very lovely.

He nodded to her across the room then sauntered out onto the terrace for some air and privacy. The end of the terrace was nicely dark and he stepped into the shadows and rested against the house wall.

What to do about Redding?

Although he asked himself the question at least twice a week, his previous answers had always been to do nothing, but as his birthday drew closer he was starting to feel his age. Five and forty was almost old. Was he going to wait 'till his sword was wrinkled and wouldn't rise before he satisfied his craving for Francis Redding?

That image was not appealing. He wasn't a vain man by any stretch of the imagination, but he'd tried to maintain a robust physique to please his lovers. To his credit, he was fitter than most lords his age, maybe not as strong as Francis. How his footman maintained his strength when he stood about for most of his day eluded Ambrose but he would ask eventually. If he was here tonight he would ask right now and then perhaps he could draw him into this dark seclusion for a kiss.

It was a constant wish.

A footstep scuffed the tiles to his left, Ambrose turned his head and cursed under his breath at the sight of Lord Silas peering into the shadows. He flattened his back hard against the cold wall and held his breath. Unfortunately, Lord Silas had excellent eyesight. He strode confidently into the shadows and stopped a pace too close for comfort. "Waiting for someone?"

"Just taking in some air." He moved away from the wall to get past Silas but was stopped by his touch.

The man's fingertips came to rest on his belly and he caressed him. "Don't go yet. We could do very well together, you and I. I would bring you great pleasure. It would be my honor."

Although Ambrose's libido fought to be satisfied,

tempting him to consider the offer, an unnatural light lit Silas' eye. He shook his head. Silas was not speaking of affection or love in their future relationship. He looked for ownership and pride in seducing a duke, an achievement to lift his consequence.

Ambrose batted the hand from his body. "I doubt that." He had to stop this decisively. "I get everything I need elsewhere," he lied. "I don't need another."

Silas frowned. "You don't need to pretend with me, Your Grace. Everyone knows you're searching for an experienced lover, someone uninhibited who will bend to your every desire without question. I can do that."

He laughed at his reputation. "Boy, you do not know the first thing about me. I enjoy a good argument and honesty. So, I will be honest with you. You do not tempt me the slightest and I wish you to leave me be. Now," he glanced around them. "I shall bid you a good evening."

Although Silas was still scowling, Ambrose did not care. He stepped through the terrace doors and wound his way back into the ballroom. Perhaps Mrs. Banks might care to dance and then he could ask her about her new beau, Singleton. If her son's story was true, he would expend the effort to gently tease her. He quite enjoyed seeing mature women blush prettily.

But Mrs. Banks was just leaving the dance floor, frantically fanning herself and red faced with Singleton by her side. On a whim, Ambrose diverted and gathered up glasses of punch for her, the grinning Lord Singleton and one for himself. If he could fan the flames of a budding romance he would consider the night a success.

Juggling the three glasses, he turned about and crashed into a wide male chest, accidentally spilling the sticky beverage all over the fellow in the process. He looked up into Lord Fletcherly's face and grimaced. Fletcherly turned a mottled red. "How dare you," he hissed.

Ambrose took a pace back. The man was overly angry about the spilled drinks for his countenance to be so dark so soon. He looked about them. What the devil was wrong with him? It was an accident, nothing more. "I apologize. Damned clumsy of me. Send me the bill for your tailor and I'll settle it immediately."

Fletcherly scowled, eyes flicking to where Lord Silas stood immobile a few feet behind him. "You will pay the bill and then some."

The crowd around them gasped. Surely the fellow wasn't about to call him out over punch? Utter nonsense. He turned away, flicking his hands toward those lingering. The wise disappeared in a hurry, but Lord Silas Flint and Lord Fairmont lingered, eyes wide with curiosity.

"I demand satisfaction, Your Grace," Fletcherly growled.

"No, Fletcherly. You could be killed," Silas cried out.

Ambrose turned slowly, piecing together what this duel was really about. Had Fletcherly seen him and Lord Silas together on the terrace? If he had, he had the wrong impression of the exchange. Lord Silas needed a leash and manacles on his hands.

"I apologized, Fletcherly. It won't happen again."

A muscle ticked in the other man's jaw. "I'll make damn sure of that, Your Grace." He threw his glove to the floor.

Ambrose groaned. A blinding stroke of bad luck.

Lord Fairmont approached and stood at his side. "I'd be happy to stand as your second, Your Grace. It'll be like old times."

Yes, very old.

Francis splashed water over his face. Hell, what a horrible night. He'd dreamed the most hideous events as a result of last night's reading and he was starting to suspect he should give up the notion of training for a physician. He just didn't feel cold blooded enough to carry on the trade.

He wiped his face dry and stared at the book. He'd been reading accounts of treatments for madness which had twisted his dreams to nightmare proportions. The case he'd read had been a ghastly business. Imagine tying a woman up and sending little bolts of charge through her temple as a cure for her aberrant behavior. He'd spent years patching up hurts. That treatment had caused the woman greater injury and even scars to the face, and as a surgeon he couldn't imagine inflicting such harm.

He closed the book. There was always a dark side to any profession. Even footmen had challenges to master. Like avoiding contact with amorous guests who felt inclined to stick their cocks in your face when you knelt to pick up a fallen object. He would never forget the indignity of Lord Fairmont's assumption that, simply because he was Staines' footman—and Staines was his lover at that time—that he could put his cock wherever he liked.

Not even Staines did that. The duke had his rules and a few limits, but he had never forced his attentions on anyone in service under his roof. Only occasionally did Francis regret that. He had to admit he was curious about sexual relations between men. But good men, not just any amorous fellow. Staines seemed to find the activity pleasurable when he'd indulged. It always seemed to improve his mood the next day.

Unfortunately for Francis, he always had knowledge of the duke's trysts. Given his standing order to remain close to the duke at all times, it was impossible to ignore the many instances when the duke sneaked away with a lover. Yet every now and then, the knowledge distressed him and he would have to exercise the notion out of his mind and body before he felt himself again. Of late, he had been exercising a great deal. It was a damned awkward life when you toiled in the duke's shadow.

Since the sky was brightening quickly, Francis dressed for riding and made his way down the main staircase to meet the duke in his study at the appointed time. His footsteps echoed in the hall but when he pushed the door open, the room was empty. Unusual. The duke slept very lightly and always woke long before Francis ever did.

He stepped out of the room and made his way up the grand staircase and along to the duke's bedchamber. He tapped on the door and waited.

When no voice or footsteps answered his knock, he eased the door open and peered into the gloom. The vast bed was empty of the duke. "Your Grace?"

No one answered. He pushed the door wider, noting the coldness of the chamber and stillness of the room. The duke had not been here this morning. His bed looked to not have been slept in at all.

He closed the door again and frowned. It was not like the duke to miss a morning ride without sending word of his change of plans. But then Francis chuckled. He wasn't the duke's wife that he had to be apologized to. He was a mere servant, one of many. Any inconvenience was hardly worth the duke's time to address.

Since Staines didn't seem likely to need him for a while yet, Francis climbed the servant's stairs to his chamber, picked up the book from last night and commenced reading about the application of electricity again.

❧

Redding was correct after all. Six o'clock *was* an ungodly hour to be about in the world.

"Gentlemen," a deep voice boomed. "I'll count to ten and then you may turn and fire when ready."

Ambrose looked up at the new dawn rising on the dew-damp green fields and cursed his stupid luck. Redding would kill him for this unfortunate situation. But he was a gentleman and, when challenged to a duel, a true gentleman had to defend his innocence against an unfounded charge.

"One."

He moved away from his opponent with a heavy heart. It had been years since he'd actually fought a duel, but at least, that time, the charge had had some merit. What was her name? Ah, yes, Angelique Montague—a vivacious and exciting woman, but a married one with a possessive husband who had not liked to share her charms with strangers despite her claim he wouldn't mind.

"Two."

The last challenge Redding had stopped by threatening his opponent's family. Ambrose did not condone that sort of thing normally, yet his opponent had been unhinged, frothing at the mouth like a savage animal and unable to be reasoned with. Redding had saved his hide more than once but he wasn't here to render the same service today. The surgeon Fairmont had insisted be sent for had failed to appear.

"Three."

Damn it all. He missed bloody Redding on his days off. He never got into scrapes like this when his servant was around. Lord Silas would never have approached him if Redding had been in attendance last night. *That's it, his days off are cancelled.*

"Four."

And if Redding had been where he was supposed to be then Fletcherly, Lord Silas' apparently secret and jealous lover, would never have thrown down his glove and started this ridiculous farce over nothing more than a mere flirtatious conversation. Who the hell dueled over ownership of male lovers anyway? He'd be the laughing stock of London. His family would be mortified.

"Five."

Now, where to aim? A body hit or should he delope? Fletcherly didn't seem the kind to not do his all to protect his interests and he'd started this. Ambrose surely had to fire back at the other man.

"Six."

The thigh? A man could bleed out and die if a main artery was hit. Redding would surely advise not to aim there. Ambrose should have sent for Redding, after all. The stomach presented the widest target, except a shot to the belly was often a lingering, painful death. He might not care if Fletcherly lived or died but he did not like a man to suffer. Damn Redding to hell and back. Thanks to his surgeoning, Ambrose knew far too much about how to cause death in an opponent. It made for a sticky conscience.

"Seven."

Four and forty was too young an age to die. He had a birthday coming up soon. There were still so many things he wanted to do before he joined his wife in heaven, if he could get in. If not for Redding's stubborn streak at keeping him out of trouble, he'd surely be there already.

"Eight."

And there was Redding to worry about. His man would not like to find another employer. Redding would miss him.

"Nine."

Time's up.

"Ten."

Ambrose turned, raising his left arm as he moved. A shot rang out and he staggered back. His chest burned and he squinted along his wavering limb to find his opponent. But he could not focus. The world tilted and he fell to his knees.

Voices rose to shouting then dimmed to a dull roar. He raised his pistol again, sighting Fletcherly at last, but his hand shook uncontrollably. His pistol fired, the ball landing heaven knew where. He closed his eyes and the ground rose up to meet him. Long blades of grass entered his nose, but he lacked the will to move his head aside or the ability to complain about the sensation.

Rough hands turned him over and the world grew dim.

God damn it. He would miss Redding.

CHAPTER FOUR

Francis bolted down the main staircase as four grooms carried the duke's still body through the front doors with Lord Fairmont bringing up the rear. "What the hell happened?"

Four pale faces met his stare, worry in each expression. The closest groom answered. "A duel, Mr. Redding. He wouldn't send for you to attend him."

He gritted his teeth over a moan as he sighted the bloody mark on the Duke of Staines' cream silk waistcoat. The ball looked to have pierced his chest and the duke's face had paled. He looked dead.

Frantically, he searched for signs of life, holding his ear over the duke's mouth and waited for breath or sensation. A faint breeze stirred across his ear. He grabbed the duke's cold hand and clasped his wrist. A pulse, weak but constant, pumped under his fingers.

Unspeakable relief surged through him. There was still a chance to save him. "Get him upstairs and into bed as gently as you can. Angus, fetch my bag from my chamber and have the housekeeper supply linen for bandages. Quickly man. The duke's life hangs in the balance."

Perhaps a bit dramatic, but Francis had learned long ago people needed firm instructions during uncertain times, especially when the duke was injured. He followed the agonizing progress of his for-once-silent master up the grand staircase and into the largest bedchamber of the townhouse. The furnishings in the duke's apartments cost a small fortune and he winced that his master's blood would once again turn the pristine white and gold bedding to scarlet.

A moan escaped the duke's lips as he was settled on the wide bed.

Fairmont rushed forward and captured the duke's hand. "I'm here, Staines."

Francis flicked his hands at the milling grooms, sending them away as the butler appeared with the tools of the surgeon's trade he kept in the house.

Angus wrung his hands as he stared at the still form on the bed. "Will he die?"

A yawning void opened at Francis' feet. He could not imagine his life without the duke smack dab in the middle of it, creating one catastrophe after another. "Not if I can help it. But have Lord Bracknell sent for immediately."

Angus paled and hurried out again.

Fairmont turned from the duke. "Surely it shan't come to that."

Bracknell was rarely in a good humor with his father. *Nothing to be done about it now.* He wouldn't be a party to any deception about the duke's health.

Francis shrugged out of his coat, his mind turning to what he had to do to save his master from yet another folly. "His son will want to know. Bracknell sent word yesterday he had arrived in Town. If you don't mind, my lord, I have work to do. Could you please wait outside?"

Fairmont looked set to argue, but he suddenly sagged. "Send word to Fairmont house. I must break the news to my wife gently and prepare her."

He held in a snort of derision. Some friend Fairmont was to the duke. *Couldn't even be bothered to wait around for the outcome.*

Lord Fairmont was replaced by the housekeeper, her arms stacked with linen. "Oh, my lord, don't take him yet," she cried at the sight of the duke's deathly pallor, and then set to ripping the linen into bandages while she mumbled a prayer.

Francis prayed along with the housekeeper as he pulled scissors from his bag. Judging by the location and amount of blood on the duke's clothes, he'd need all the help of divine intervention he could get. He turned and methodically cut the duke's clothing from his upper body to see what he had to deal with.

Although a dark stain marred the perfection of the muscled chest, Francis breathed a sigh of relief. The injury could be far enough from the heart and lungs to prove less dangerous than he'd first feared. There was only possibility of infection and blood loss to counter. Both of which could still kill his duke.

The housekeeper cleared her throat as she picked up the duke's shredded clothing. "Is there anything else, sir?"

"Not yet. You may wait outside until I call for you." The servants did not like to see him at work and their gasping and fainting was often a great distraction. He worked better alone and was grateful when the woman closed the door behind her.

The duke's eyes fluttered open, their gaze unfocussed. "Are they all gone?"

"Mrs. McClurry just stepped out," Francis murmured, lifting a wadded cravat used to stop the bleeding clear of the wound to see the worst of it. Blood welled slowly to the surface.

"Good, she can pray for my soul at a distance." The duke swallowed. "How bad?"

"Bad enough that I cannot possibly scold you. Yet." He lifted the long chain that hung from the duke's neck and stared at the late duchess' ring attached to it. Francis rubbed his fingertips over the expensive bauble then lifted the piece to the duke's line of sight and then to the duke's lips. "For luck."

The duke kissed the ring and Francis' fingers, too, and then closed his eyes.

A tight lump formed in his throat. Francis left the duke to scrub his hands and collect his instruments. He willed calm to replace his anxiety. He could not let the duke die from any mistake he made. He had to remain in control and dispassionate as he dug into the duke's flesh. His life depended on it.

Calmer, he picked up forceps, laid them beside the duke's fluttering chest and braced himself to dig for the ball lodged in the duke's chest.

As he took a breath, the duke curled his left arm around his thigh.

Francis frowned. "Do you want me to cause you

greater pain? Should I have you restrained?"

A ghost of a smile crossed the duke's lips. "Just wanted one last pleasant memory before I forget why I like you. This is bound to hurt even if I die in the end."

"You're not going to die, Your Grace. Only the good die young." Francis nudged the duchess' ring with his smallest finger to prove his point. The duchess had been a remarkable lady and had died far too young. The household staff still marked her birthday with a silent toast: the duke marked her death in a dark mood.

"And I'm far from good nowadays." The duke squeezed Francis' backside. "Ask me to repay you properly when you've saved my life again. I'm sure we can come to some mutually pleasurable arrangement."

Francis sighed. "Only you could proposition someone while you're bleeding to death." He leaned close to the duke's ear. "Ambrose Manning, if you don't stop groping me and distracting me from saving your life I can promise you you'll never use your cock again. I know you're afraid but let go. Trust me."

"Always trust you." The duke's lips quivered. "Will you let me put my cock anywhere I like after you've saved my life if I comply?"

He frowned at the absurd question. "You already do."

"No, I don't. I don't put it in you," Staines whispered. "And I'm regretting I haven't rather badly just now."

Francis gasped at the blunt confession. The duke's eyes remained closed, although he still k kneaded Francis' backside, fingertips dipping into the crack of his arse with disturbing agility. Was he not as ill as he made out?

Yet his life's blood seeped from his chest with startling persistence.

The duke sighed; his hand lost its strength. "Don't let me forget, Red."

Francis tucked the duke's arms tightly under the sheeting to keep him still in preparation for the surgery. He also pushed the duke's proposition from his mind. Now was not the time to think of any of that nonsense. The duke would likely ignore his bold suggestion when he was well again.

He slowed his breathing as he positioned the forceps and probed the gaping bloody hole for the ball.

The duke swore.

Francis dug a little deeper. The duke groaned and whimpered. But he could not avoid inflicting pain. The ball had to come out and soon. The forceps scraped over metal.

The duke howled in agony. "Fucking hell, Redding, you bastard. If you don't get that ball out of me in the next moment, you can consider yourself unemployed."

Francis ignored the duke's outburst and attempted to capture the ball once more. His employment had been terminated too many times in the past for him to get concerned about it yet. He'd only believe the duke if he said it while he wasn't under duress.

He had it secure when the duke stiffened suddenly, and then slumped in a faint. But that was a relief for Redding since he could not give the duke any potion for the pain. The duke hadn't the head for the usual pain relief afforded by laudanum. And Redding would never go through the trauma of ending the duke's addiction to the opiate again, as he had during the early years after the duchess had died in childbirth.

He pulled the small round free and placed it on his palm, then rolled the ball around with the tip of his finger, coating his palm with the duke's blood as he checked that it hadn't shattered against bone on impact. Luckily, he had the whole of it.

He set it aside and mopped carefully at the blood seeping from the gaping hole. His work was far from done. He still had to find the missing piece of the duke's shirt.

The bedchamber doors burst open. "What the hell has he done now?"

Francis didn't look up as the duke's eldest son, Lord Bracknell, stormed into the room without knocking, but continued to search the bloody mess for fragments of fine linen. He peered at the shirt again, comparing the gap with the pieces he found and dug deeper. "He's trying not to die, my lord."

Bracknell gagged and coughed and staggered away from the bed. "You mean you are trying to keep my foolish father in one piece. How did this happen?"

Francis studied the material again and let out a sigh of relief that he had filled the gap. "I was not with the duke at the time, but I am told he dueled this morning." He spared Lord Bracknell a glance, and then nodded. "It appears far worse than it may be. As long as infection does not set in he should be up and around in no time."

"More mischief." Bracknell leaned against the far wall. "Thank God we have you to patch him up and nursemaid him back into health. No other physician will tolerate his ways."

Francis chuckled, a nervous relief from the stress of moments ago. "I believe he's ended my employment again so you may have to send out enquiries."

Bracknell frowned, a perplexed expression on his face. "Again?"

Francis pressed a square of linen against the wound to sop up the blood. "My eighth termination, I believe."

A wicked grin crossed Bracknell's face. "Would you care for another position, Redding?"

He frowned, as he reached for needle and thread in preparation for stitching the duke's chest back together. "Now is hardly the time." Really, Bracknell had been much easier to deal with when he was in short pants and had half Francis' height. He'd grown into a man much like his father—far too impatient with life to take heed of the gravity of a situation. Francis threaded the needle and lifted the cloth from the wound.

"When he's silent is the perfect time for any reasonable conversation," Bracknell continued from the far side of the room. "I want to employ you as the family physician."

Francis shook his head. "I'm only a surgeon, as you can see. A physician has to be registered with the Royal College of Physicians and does not tend to wounds like this. He is a gentleman. I'm hardly that. My father was a farmer as you well know."

"Stuff and nonsense." Bracknell paced the chamber. "You are a bloody good surgeon, by all accounts. I do not want to lose your services. If my father keeps firing you we could do just that. You would work for me, but reside here with him, until I have need of you. Father cannot boot you any further than my residence."

A very tempting offer, one Francis wished he might take up, but there was always a problem to be faced when dealing with those socially above you—they never noticed the problems for someone with his low connections. "You are still forgetting the examination I must sit. I know none of the examiners and what they will ask of me."

Bracknell dismissed Francis' valid concern with a wave of his hand. "Pendergast is a good friend. He'll help me get you licensed in exchange for my patronage."

Francis watched the wound and, when he was satisfied the bleeding had slowed sufficiently to cause him little concern, he dusted it with Dragon's Blood. If Bracknell would just go away he'd be done with the duke directly. "Forgive me for being dense this morning after digging into your father's shoulder, but if I'm employed here how could that possibly benefit you?"

Bracknell set his hands to his hips. "It has come to my attention my father behaves far better when you are around to keep him in line. I spoke to my Uncle Lynton at Christmas and he believes that to be true too. Last night is the perfect example of what happens when you're absent from any society event. Yet, I'm fully aware my father can order any servant away and get himself shot at the next morning. However, Dr. Francis Redding will be a gentleman and free to ignore His Grace should he chose to. I'm hoping you will disobey him quite often and follow him about mercilessly."

Francis closed his mouth in shock. This didn't appear to be a sudden decision on Bracknell's part. He looked to have been considering the matter for months and consulting the duke's family into the bargain. Utter foolishness. "I won't be invited to the same events, my lord. What you suggest is not the answer you need.

Perhaps you should find His Grace a wife. Your mother kept him well-satisfied."

He returned his attention to the wound, ready to insert the first stitch and to bandage the duke's chest shortly after that. Very carefully, Francis pierced the duke's skin and drew the wound together with two knotted threads. Thankfully, Bracknell remained silent while he worked and he was pleased with the neat result. He dusted the wound again and laid a fresh square of linen lightly over the injury.

"He doesn't need a wife when he has you," Bracknell murmured from a new position at Francis' shoulder. "Don't worry about the details. I'll see to it that your name is on the guest lists of all the society matrons before the month is out."

Francis shook his head. "Forgive me, my lord, but you're as mad as your father."

Instead of being offended, Bracknell laughed. "That's what I like about you, *Dr.* Redding. You are not afraid to speak your mind to any one of us Mannings. No wonder he can't live without you. Look, he's awake and listening."

CHAPTER FIVE

"Rupert, stop bothering my servant." Ambrose winced at the sharp sting that pierced his chest when he spoke. Gods, getting shot was a trial to recover from.

"Lie still," Redding urged, his hot hands sliding gently over Ambrose to restrain him.

Despite his pain, a little thrill shot through him at the sensation. "I would be still if you two would stop blathering," he gasped. Carefully, he opened his eyes and met Redding's worried gaze. "Well?"

Redding didn't smile. "Now, we wait."

Damn it all, that meant nothing good if Redding didn't reassure him instantly. His footman would never lie to him though and give him false hope. He gritted his teeth as he shifted his shoulder carefully and saw stars.

When he opened his eyes again, his son moved into his line of vision. "Who was it, Father?"

Ambrose pressed his lips together. He wasn't about to confess anything to his son about last night or this morning. He had faith his second would hold his tongue, even if Rupert was a particularly insistent boy.

Redding slid his hands off his chest and Ambrose missed the warmth instantly. He was cold all over. Any minute his teeth would surely chatter. He clenched his jaw tight to prevent that from happening in front of his son.

"Could this wait until later, Lord Bracknell?" Redding asked. "I'm hardly done tending His Grace's injury. I'd rather he rest for a while yet."

While Rupert didn't look pleased about it, he nodded. "I'll remain here in the house. Send word to the library if he becomes difficult."

"Thank you, my lord." Redding nodded. "But I believe I can manage him."

The door closed with a soft click. "That's the quickest

you've ever gotten rid of him, Red. I owe you another guinea."

Redding turned abruptly from the bed. "Oh, shut up."

He followed Redding's movements, a little shocked by his outburst. His footman strode to a washbasin and scrubbed ruthlessly at his hands. Then he set them to the table top and his knuckles turned white as they clutched the wood. Ambrose gulped nervously. Redding was upset. Yet he straightened again in the next moment, turned and marched back across the room to where Ambrose laid waiting.

His expression had blanked of all emotion. "This needs dressing properly."

Ambrose hated when Redding got like this—cold and unfeeling—as if he were merely an unfamiliar person bleeding before him. *Professional indifference*, Redding had once called it. They were hardly a stranger to each other's moods and whims. They'd rattled about in each other's company more than half their lives and Ambrose knew without a doubt that Redding was furious with him. Yet he would barely show it.

Ambrose nodded the tiniest amount. "Of course."

Slowly and very carefully, Redding wrapped Ambrose's torso in linen and he was settled comfortably as he could be in his vast bed. It had taken all of Ambrose's fortitude not to cry out against the sharp pain as he was jostled.

He wiped his upper lip with his good arm until Redding took over the task with a square of linen. He met Redding's gaze. "Thank you, Red."

Redding brushed a hand over his hair in a rare, soft gesture of affection. "Damned fool. Whose wife was it this time?"

"Not a wife." Ambrose gulped, tasting the metallic flavor of blood on his tongue. "Can I wash this foul taste from my mouth?"

His footman didn't ask again about Ambrose's latest indiscretion as he returned and held a small glass of sherry to Ambrose's lips.

As his head fell back to the pillow, Ambrose gasped. "A misunderstanding. I promise you." It was suddenly very important that Redding know the gossip would be unfounded. He would hear of the matter eventually, Redding always did, and Ambrose would not like him to get the wrong impression. Although, society believed he had dueled over a glass of spilled punch, he had fought for his honor against a jealous man. He had not encouraged Lord Silas the way Lord Fletcherly imagined. He didn't find the fool attractive at all.

What he wanted, more than anything, was to test the waters with Redding, despite his own hesitation. He had decided that as he lay dying.

"They always are." A harsh sigh passed his footman's lips. "I'll distract Lord Bracknell from the matter for as long as I can."

Ambrose slipped his arm around Redding's thigh and squeezed. "I'd appreciate that. I—"

The door burst open again as Mrs. Banks stormed the room, her son trailing behind. Ambrose quickly loosened his grip and Redding made a good show of checking his pulse to hide what he'd been doing. One did not fondle another man before a lady.

"Good Lord, it is true? Is he dead?"

A painful laugh bubbled from his lips. "Not yet, Mrs. Banks. However, I have an excellent surgeon to tend me. Come back tomorrow for tea and see if I've expired."

Redding crossed the room and herded Mrs. Banks from the chamber, speaking low and confidently about his eventual recovery. Ambrose wasn't sure he believed those words, but appreciated the comfort the man offered the excitable Mrs. Banks. Redding closed the door behind her with a quiet word, and then locked it for good measure.

"Alone at last," Ambrose whispered as Redding crossed to the windows and drew the drapes closed against the bright day. "Not even my valet about. What did you do to Smith?"

Redding picked up a heavy, comfortable armchair as if it were weightless and set it close beside the bed. "Nothing. There was blood involved and he disappeared immediately. With luck the little fool won't return."

A grin tugged Ambrose's lips, but with the drapes drawn and the room darker he was suddenly very weary. "You really don't like him, do you?"

"The man spends more time admiring you and your possessions than performing his duties."

Was Francis just the tiniest bit jealous? Hope and excitement sent his pulse climbing. Ambrose held out his good hand. "I never noticed."

After a time, Redding's wide palm slid over his and squeezed. "Enough. You should rest, Your Grace."

Rest seemed a very good idea. He closed his eyes. "I much prefer it when you slip and call me by my given name. Reminds me of when we were boys running wild by the river on the estate when my father wasn't looking. It's been a long time since we've been fishing, Red."

"A very long time ago now, but you never enjoyed fishing, if you remember. You slept on the riverbank or watched me at it." Redding's grip changed as he tugged the armchair closer to the bed, but he didn't let go of Ambrose's hand. "Be still, Ambrose, and do your best to heal quickly. It won't be long before the whole *ton* comes trouping through those doors to get a look at you. You'd better rest while you can."

Gads, they surely would try it, wouldn't they? Not even a near death experience would give him privacy to heal with only Redding to see his suffering. He shifted closer to Redding and sighed at how short a time the peace would last.

Francis woke with a start as someone nudged his shoulder. He opened his eyes to find himself lying face down against the duke's thigh and the duke caressing his hair. The situation was so unexpected that he simply stared at the duke instead of moving away from the caress. That Staines was finally awake after a week of uncertainty possibly accounted for his stupor. He'd been in and out of consciousness since the first day after the duel and it was a relief to see his gaze had cleared somewhat. He no longer thrashed in pain, and his skin glowed with greater health.

A slow grin twisted his employer's lips. "You are a very heavy sleeper, Red. I did not know that about you."

"Forgive me." Francis jumped up and checked the duke's wound and temperature. Staines did not appear feverish anymore and he let out a heavy sigh as he tucked the blankets higher around him where they had slipped down to expose the wide expanse of his chest.

The duke moved a hand up and down Francis' thigh. "I'm thirsty." Staines licked his lips.

Cursing his foolishness for sleeping when he should have been watchful, Francis rushed around the chamber to get water and open the drapes. When he came back to the duke's side, his master was squinting.

Staines gulped down the liquid and wiped a hand over his mouth. "Thank you."

An urgent tapping sounded on the door and Francis scowled at the noise.

"Someone has been doing that for a while. Do we have to answer them?"

He groaned. "It is probably Lord Bracknell or Lord Fairmont come to check on you. They have been here every day demanding to see you."

Staines gestured to his partially covered chest and grimaced. "Well, whoever it is can wait a little longer. I'm hardly presentable."

"You want to dress? Now?" Francis set his hands to his hips. "For Gods sake, Ambrose, you almost died. Appearances can go to the devil."

The grin that twisted the duke's face was at complete odds to his precarious health. "Now Red, don't be losing your temper with me. I cannot look as if I was at death's door. Think of the gossip."

Francis threw his hands up in the air and stormed across the room to the duke's closet. Foolishness. More utter bloody foolishness. He ran his hands over the racks of clothing and selected what the duke would require: silk waistcoat, fine linen shirt, and a handful of cravats with an expensive pin to stick into the final one.

When he emerged, the duke raised a brow. "We could have called for my valet to attend to my dressing."

Francis scowled. He did not want to be alone with the duke and Smith and witness the valet ogling their employer. The sight always put him in a very bad mood, and he was still annoyed at the duke over the duel. He dropped a waistcoat on the bed, but took the shirt toward a side table. Then, to improve his mood, he took the scissors to it and sliced open the back so the garment would not need to be pulled over his head.

When he was finished, the duke chuckled. "So you're not keen on that shirt I take it?"

"If you are going to dress to meet with a bunch of fools then I am not about to destroy my work in the process. This will cause you less pain." Francis stated. He held the shirt out to the duke so he could see what he meant.

"Imminently practical, Red."

Gingerly, Francis slid the sleeve over the duke's right arm, then over his left and tucked the edges beneath the duke's body snugly. He buttoned the shirt at the neck and then reached for a cravat. He had little practice with dressing the duke, or tying the intricate knots the man favored, but the duke would have to accept his efforts or forget about this absurdity altogether.

Staines raised his head without argument so Francis could loop the long length around his neck. But he gasped as his shoulder was jostled and gripped Francis' leg as he tied the first knot securely.

"Sorry," he muttered.

"It's nothing. You are very gentle with me."

"I take pride in doing my best, Your Grace."

Staines rubbed the leg with more pressure. "Your Grace, again. Can we not be simply Ambrose and Francis when we are alone together?"

"You usually call me Red." He frowned. "Besides, that would not be proper, Your Grace. I should not like to overstep."

The duke's touch traveled up his arm and gripped his bicep, preventing him from completing the knot. "You may overstep with me at any time, Francis. I would welcome you with open arms."

Francis drew back. "Did you hit your head hard on the ground after you were shot?"

"Not that I remember."

Concerned, Francis softly ran his hands over the duke's skull, feeling for additional lumps he'd missed to explain this odd conversation. When he found nothing, he peered into the duke's face. But Staines had closed his eyes, his breathing rough. "Are you unwell?"

The duke's eyes snapped open. "If this is unwell then you may treat me at any time. Do you have no idea of what your touch does to me?"

CHAPTER SIX

Staines swallowed hard as the intimate proximity to his footman stirred his lust to dangerous levels. Every time was the same. He wanted more from their association than he should and by God, he was heartily sick of fighting the feeling. He pulled Francis closer until his breath brushed over his lips.

Francis' eyes widened. "Your Grace?"

"Oh, shut up."

He kissed him full on the mouth. "That is for saving my sorry hide from my own idiocy." He kissed him again. "That was for all the past times you have done the very same and I never thanked you properly." He brushed his lips across Francis' gently, tempted to try for a deeper kiss. "And that is my promise to never do anything so foolish again. I am sorry to have worried you."

Francis drew back suddenly, gaze flying to the doorway where someone was knocking with annoying rapidity. He wiped a hand over his lips.

Ambrose winced at the gesture and looked away. It had been a foolish wish Francis would want him in return and, mortified, he buried his lust as quickly as he could.

His footman left the bed, and then he heard the snipping of scissors destroying another fine garment. He sighed. He was quite alone in his admiration, it seemed. He should have guessed this attraction to Francis would come to naught. Except that he truly admired Francis Redding and not just lusted after him.

He had for the longest time.

Perhaps it was cowardly, but he closed his eyes, and kept them closed as Francis returned to the bed. He could not stand to see the disgust that might linger in the man's eyes and he lay unresisting as his footman finished dressing him in his altered waistcoat without a word. The pin was carefully inserted into his cravat without causing the slightest tug on his shoulder. The tapping on the door grew to a steady pounding.

"I'll see who it is now," Francis murmured, smoothing the blankets over Ambrose one last time and stirring up his lust again.

He opened his eyes as Francis strode across the room. He admired the strength hidden behind proper clothing and lamenting that he'd never learn the contours of his skin.

Francis spoke quietly to his son, Rupert, and then set the door wide. His second from the duel, Lord Fairmont, weaved across the chamber with Lord Silas hot on his heels.

"Had to see for myself." Fairmont squinted at him. "Was sure you were done for. Bracknell, here, assures me you are on the mend."

Fairmont was quite drunk, by the look of his bloodshot eyes and sound of his slurred speech. Ambrose pasted a smile on his lips. "Takes more than one duel to rid society of me. Come back tomorrow for luncheon with your wife." When Francis' brow rose in disbelief, he could feel a blush building. Perhaps it was too soon to entertain, even on a modest scale, but he needed to ensure that Fairmont would hold his tongue about the duel. "Let us make it the day after. I've forgotten a prior engagement."

Lord Silas edged closer, his fingers grazing Ambrose's thigh out of sight of Lord Fairmont and his son. "I'm sure you'll be back to your old tricks in no time and back among society where you belong. Everyone is talking about you."

Unfortunately, Francis saw the caress from Lord Silas. His eyes widened unnaturally then his expression turned cold and flat. He turned his attention to his instruments on a far table.

"Yes, in no time at all." What the devil was Francis doing? He was placing everything into his little bag in a rush. "You may assure our mutual acquaintance he did not kill a duke this week and the duke holds no grudge for the misunderstanding. Be sure to set him straight, won't you?"

"He's fled London. I tried to explain gently, but he would not listen," Lord Silas said as he sank onto the bed beside him with a heavy thump.

Ambrose winced as the bed was jostled enough to effect him.

Lord Fairmont laughed, quite missing Lord Silas' morose expression and Ambrose's wince of pain. "I'd be running too. What a fool to call a man out over a spilled glass of punch and to fire early. I'm surprised you accepted the duel in the first place."

Beyond Fairmont, Francis shook his head.

"A man must defend his honor." Ambrose met and held Lord Silas' gaze until the young lord's skin pinked with discomfort. "I'll take his retreat as his resignation from the Hunt Club, and yours too, for that matter. You had the power to stop him and didn't. I do not spill punch indiscriminately."

Fairmont's bloodshot eyes widened, his gaze flickering to Lord Silas in shock as he fathomed out the events that led up to the duel. His lip curled in distaste as he looked between Ambrose and Silas.

Lord Silas jumped from the bed. "I'm sure there is no need for such decisions to be made now. You should rest. Another time, Your Grace."

He would not forgive Lord Silas for making a fool out of him. The man would be punished by exclusion from the Hunt Club as, of course, would Fletcherly. He'd never stand the ridiculous pair in his presence again. He glanced beyond them as Francis pulled on his coat. Damn it, Francis was going to leave him alone. Ambrose needed him to stay. He turned to his unwanted guests. "Good day to you both. Fairmont, don't forget to come Friday for luncheon."

Fairmont looked to the floor. "My wife may be busy Friday. I'll let you know," he said softly.

He goggled. Did Fairmont really think he'd wanted to duel over a man like Lord Silas? Had his friend become that big a fool? "Send word when you can."

Fairmont and Silas left and Rupert closed the door after them.

Reluctantly, Ambrose looked over at his footman, but he could not tell what the man was thinking or feeling. He was lost in his own thoughts, one hand stroking over the bag's metal clasp. Never a good sign, that kind of thing.

"The duel, Father." Rupert pressed against the bed. "I want the details now."

"No," Francis growled.

Ambrose blinked in surprise at Francis' loud denial.

Unfortunately, Rupert was not so calm about it. He stalked up to Francis and glowered. "Who the hell do you think you are to interfere? This is between my father and me."

"I am no one and never have been, but I am heartily sick of the pair of you. Your father could have died but you, of course, had to demand all the sordid details of the duel before he was well again. And you," Francis rounded on Ambrose. "Can you never keep out of trouble for even one night?"

Ambrose blinked at the set-down and couldn't think of what to say. The events leading up to the duel weren't even his fault. But he did chase pleasure as often as he could, usually in an attempt to deny how much he wanted Francis Redding. Occasionally, he got into trouble for it. But Francis didn't know his reasons. The minute he got him alone again he would explain everything and see where they stood. Hopefully still together, or at least as near friends. He was clear headed enough to acknowledge he might never get a chance for more.

"You go too far, Redding," Rupert hissed. If only his son knew the danger he was in. Francis could whip him in three moves if he wished to. "There are many who covet your position here. No one is irreplaceable."

"Rupert," Ambrose barked in alarm. "That is not your decision to make. It is mine. Redding remains."

Francis ignored him and grabbed his bag. "I do not go far enough. I'm sick of cleaning up your mistakes too,

Lord Bracknell. You can choke on your own consequence for all I care."

"Francis!" he called, but his footman was out the door without a backward glance and didn't bother to return. Ambrose tried to rise. Sharp pain shot through his chest and he collapsed to the pillow gasping.

Rupert sat with a thump, jostling Ambrose enough to make him grit his teeth. Was Francis the only one who gave a damn if he was injured? That seemed very likely so far. He glared at his son. "What the hell did you do that for?"

Rupert jumped to his feet like a guilty school boy. "I didn't do anything."

"Oh, really?" Ambrose scowled. "Then why, pray tell, is Francis not here where he belongs?"

Rupert set his hands to his hips. "Why do you care? You ended his employment again, I'm told."

He groaned. "Must have been when he took the ball out. I don't remember. He knows better than to believe me. I fire him every other year, but it's always when I'm injured and when he's stitching me up."

Rupert shook his head. "Are you sure of that, Father, because he was definitely tempted by my intention to employ him as the family physician."

Ambrose studied his son. Rupert didn't lie well, at least not to him, so the conversation about Francis leaving his service must have happened while he'd been insensible. A tight knot of apprehension twisted his insides. Francis couldn't leave his position. He couldn't bear that thought. He swallowed. "Did he say he accepted?"

"No, he told me I was mad like you. I'm having second thoughts about offering the position now. He'd always seemed so respectful and obliging in the past. Can't employ a man who resents us."

A wave of uncertainty swept over him. Francis had revealed all kinds of emotions today that the man usually kept to himself. Although he'd give his health to discover the depths of those emotions, he latched on to the greatest threat to his happiness. "Why do you think

Francis wants to be a physician?"

In answer, Rupert lifted an unfamiliar book from a nearby table. *Annals of Insanity.* "He's been reading this all week. I'll speak to Redding about his outburst and decide what to do about his service. I'll take care of everything."

If Francis became a physician, he would have ample means to support himself. He would have a better position in society and would not be around anymore. Ambrose clutched the sheets. "No, you will not. Francis Redding has been at my side since I was a boy. He helped me resurrect the estate after Father did his best to ruin us and stood by me when your mother died. If he wants more from life then I will gladly do for him what I can. He deserves some latitude. He is more a companion to me than a servant, and you will say nothing about his outburst. For God's sake, could you prod and sew up your oldest acquaintance without feeling just a might unnerved by the experience?"

"I suppose it could have been quite difficult for him," Rupert conceded. "He's barely left your side since you were injured. Pendergast offered to assist, but Redding wouldn't allow him near you with even laudanum. Thought Redding would strike him at one point when he tried to get close to the bed. Pendergast won't come back."

The thought of laudanum on his tongue, of white-smoke filling his lungs, sent a shot of yearning through his body briefly. But then he remembered the dark days after his wife's death and what Redding had done to end the drug's hold on his mind—the risks he had taken on his own to bring Ambrose back from oblivion. No one could learn Redding had tied him up in his bedchamber at Tindel Park and denied him liberty until he was a rational man again.

It was a period of his life he didn't like to examine too closely and neither he nor Redding had discussed the matter again. He would never have recovered if Redding hadn't been an utter tyrant about the matter and insisted he live.

"I cannot have the opiate, Rupert. Redding did the right thing to deny Pendergast." He swallowed uncomfortably. "He has worried for me as much as you. Could you imagine what would happen to him if I died from this injury? He took a great risk attending me himself. Regardless of whether he did his best work, he would be blamed should I perish."

"But he is a surgeon." Rupert waved his hand. "He would be used to death by now."

Ambrose didn't think so. Not after seeing Francis after he'd attended Miss Felicity before he was shot. He'd seemed bone tired and Ambrose had been worried by his expression. Perhaps he asked too much from him. "I don't believe that to be the case, Rupert. He doesn't even keep the fish he catches. He tosses them back most times."

Rupert's frown grew. "You are overly familiar with him, Father. You've become blind to his faults. No servant should behave as he does."

"And I have misbehaved more than my share, too. Leave Redding alone."

"Well," Rupert pushed to his feet. "Since my assistance is not wanted here, I will take my leave of you, Father. Do let me know should you be inclined to die. I should like to wring my hands and wail at your passing."

He grinned to break the tension. "Cheeky cub. I'll see you tomorrow."

His son smiled reluctantly and held out his hand. "Heal fast, Papa. Society has nothing to talk about when you are not around."

Ambrose caught his son's hand and squeezed. "When Redding says I can venture out I will, and not before. Raise hell in my absence, Rupert."

His son nodded and strode toward the door. But at the door, he turned back. "About the club, Papa. If Redding insists you rest even more, will you be able to manage the affair from here? I thought he would burst a vessel when you invited Fairmont to luncheon tomorrow. How will you manage it all?"

Damn it. The club required strict supervision to run

smoothly. With everything that had happened today, he couldn't very well ask Francis to run the place. Besides, the members would never listen to him as they would obey Ambrose.

He stared at his son. Perhaps it was time to hand over the reins now and see what was left when the dust settled. Few in the family had any inkling of what went on inside the club, or of the wicked entertainments offered to patrons. Rupert may very well be furious when he learned. However, the club profits kept the duchy running smoothly during the estate's lean years and paid his son's quarterly allowance.

He could not run the club from his sick bed, and he was likely to be stuck in idleness for at least a month if the ache in his shoulder was anything to go by. But if he gave up the club management to Rupert and then Francis left his service to take up work as a physician then there was nothing left in his days worth getting out of bed for. The thought of that bleak future was worse than turning five and forty. Yet holding Francis back from fulfilling his dreams would be utterly selfish.

He gritted his teeth. When Francis got back he would apologize for the kisses, for his son, and ask him if becoming a physician was what he truly wanted. If it was, he would have his support. He owed him his life for his unwavering loyalty.

With that lowering thought in the back of his mind, Ambrose waved his arm toward Rupert to draw him back into the chamber. At least while he was injured his son might not strangle him for the potential scandal the club activities could cause him.

CHAPTER SEVEN

Francis barged through the servant's entrance and flung himself up the narrow stairs and along to his chamber at the Hunt Club. He was so angry that he had no clear memory of traversing the distance between the duke's home and the club. The only evidence was that the soles of his feet were hot and perspiration trickled down his back.

He threw himself into a hard wooden chair and dropped his head to his hands. Foolishness. The duke was almost killed over a trivial misunderstanding, and that pup Lord Silas was somehow involved, given the way he had boldly cozened up to the duke on his sick bed. He sucked in a sharp breath. Had the duke dueled over a new lover?

He must be getting old. He'd missed the signs the duke was interested in the sniveling lord. The man was trouble, no doubt about it. He thought too well of himself to be healthy. As the duke's lover, he would be a nightmare to manage. He'd likely expose the duke's bedding habits to anyone who'd listen. That could get the duke hung and could not be allowed.

Yet, Francis couldn't imagine the duke with Lord Silas. He usually favored someone nearer his own nature—muscled, confident, and someone closer in rank and consequence like Lord Fairmont had been a few years ago. He pushed the thought of the duke and his many lovers from his mind. No matter what he'd hinted at today, there was no way in hell the duke had meant a word of it. It was only his injury and fear of dying that had affected him to act out of character and say the things he had. The duke would never want a farmer's son.

He sat up as his door creaked open an inch, then widened when Marinari slipped through wearing a peacock blue gown. "What has happened? Is the duke all right?"

Francis nodded. "'Tis early days yet, but I believe he will be himself again soon."

She let out a relieved breath and drew closer. "Why are you here? Shouldn't you be attending him?"

He'd run from his own anger and frustration after guessing the cause of the duel before he really said what was on his mind. Lord Bracknell was a fine one to lecture his own father – he was just as reckless as the duke. Francis had cleaned up every mess he made without acknowledgement or question. He had no patience with hypocrites. "I needed to check on Miss Felicity."

She scowled at him. "That is not the reason and we both know that."

He raised an eyebrow. Marinari might not be an actual woman, but she possessed a woman's intuition. Her dark eyes glared and he dropped his gaze. "I feared for the duke's health should I remain."

She moved behind him, set her hands to his shoulders and squeezed. "You must be very angry to leave his side at such a time. He is careless with his affections. I do not understand why he looks elsewhere when he has you. I know I would not."

He sighed as she kneaded his tense muscles. "As I've told you before, the duke does not see me that way. But his behavior worries me more every day. He grows bolder when he should take greater care. The club has made him feel invincible." Gads, Marinari's hands worked magic. Tension fled under her determined assault. He closed his eyes to savor the short moment of simple pleasure.

Her breath tickled his ear. "Yet he does not dabble here. He goes elsewhere when any one of us would welcome him with open arms. He is said to be a man of large appetites and wicked passions. The others are disappointed no one has ever come close to tempting him and can tell us if the tales are true."

Francis moved his head, lest she attempt to kiss him as she had once before. "He has his rules, many of them.

He will not dabble with a servant who is dependent on him for their livelihood. Perhaps he should, and then I might not have to perform surgery on him so often. What am I going to do with him? I cannot watch over him every second of every day."

"Perhaps it is time you forgot *your* caution. Would the duke's life be safe from harm if he dabbled with you instead of those frivolous lords and ladies he favors?" She wrapped her arms tight about his chest and held him in place. "Perhaps you should seduce him and keep him in his own bed with you."

She laughed against his neck and Francis fought against the restraint and suggestion. Marinari was very strong. She would not release him. Her breath tickled his ear, then she pressed her lips to the skin of his jaw. Regardless of how practical her suggestion sounded, he had no idea how to go about seducing another man, let alone the duke.

He shook his head.

She laughed at his denial. "I think you could entice him easily enough. Do you see how straightforward it can be to get a man to rise? You harden for me because I am touching you. Yet you do not find me the least bit attractive under normal circumstances, do you?"

"I don't." Francis confessed. He did not find a man in women's clothing worthy of more than his surprise. It wasn't his business who did though, but his cock had thickened enough to cause a disturbing bulge in his trousers. Perhaps there was something to her words. The only man who affected him was the duke, and no other before this. "Release me."

Her deep chuckle barked through the room. "I imagine the duke would not say that to you. He may try to hide it, but his gaze follows you. He lusts for you and I saw the flare of jealousy in his eyes when he found me alone with you. I think you should do something about him before he rejoins society. What better time than when he is injured and confined to his bed."

Seduce a patient? "That's a despicable suggestion."

Marinari slid her arms from Francis and she circled

the chair to meet his gaze. "Is the duke worth it? You know his tastes, and he is fond of you. You will never know if you do not try. Just be sure to relate all the particulars when you are done. I like to keep a log of a gentleman's dimension." Her eyes dipped. "I should like to judge yours, too."

Francis batted her hand away as she reached toward the placard of his trousers. The minx was not touching him. The only man allowed would be the duke. He heaved a weary sigh. Marinari's suggestion was very tempting. Could he give the duke what he needed? He'd never know until he tried, he supposed. The same as with everything in life. He stood, suddenly uncomfortable with his thoughts. "I'll check on Felicity and be on my way."

She sauntered to the door. "Good luck. I'll leave a little package for you in here before you depart. You may find the contents useful in the days to come." She wriggled her fingers at him and swept out.

Alone again, Francis heaved a sigh and dismissed his brief moment of madness. He would not be seducing the duke this night or any other. There was no point considering the notion. He collected the few things he needed and made his way toward Felicity's chamber door. He tapped lightly, heard a deep voiced murmur, and barged his way in. "I said no visitors."

Mr. Banks sat cross-legged on the end of Miss Felicity's bed, cards and a handful of coins piled between them. Felicity looked to be winning. He quirked an eyebrow.

Felicity subsided to her pillows. "Good evening, sir."

"Miss Felicity. I do hope you've been resting."

Her gaze strayed to the young man climbing from her bed. "I've followed your instructions to the letter, and your colleague, Mr. Hibbert, should have told you I was, too. But Mr. Banks is determined to entertain me with cards during my recuperation." She slid her fingers through the pile of coins but her gaze followed Banks with an appreciative smile.

"Very good. Mr. Banks, if you wouldn't mind making yourself scarce I should like to examine the patient."

"I'd rather stay," he scowled and Francis was shocked by the possessiveness he displayed.

He put his bag on the end of the bed. "Banks, by all means stay, if Miss Felicity wishes you to do so. But this is a medical examination. I should only be a few minutes."

Felicity giggled. "Oh, do go out, Mr. Banks. Redding here has never shown an interest before this and we have been alone many a time."

Grudgingly, Banks slipped out.

Francis quirked an eyebrow at Felicity's wide smile and pulled the sheet down the bed. Her gown had already risen to her thighs and he pushed the flimsy material away. "How have you been?"

"Only a little uncomfortable, sir. Is that good?"

He drew her knees apart and squinted at her quim. "Very good. You'll be back to your tricks in no time." He pulled the night gown over her knees. "Do not let the gentlemen rush you."

"No chance of that. Mr. Banks has already reserved me for my first engagement and will wait happily until I am well again." She set her hand behind her head. "What is his reputation, Redding? What sort of man is he outside of the club?"

The glow in her face as she talked about Mr. Banks was a new one. If he didn't know her better, he might think she was smitten. "A decent sort, and one of the duke's closest acquaintances this Season. Do not engage his heart in your escapades. He is very young still."

She winked. "That was not the part I wished to engage. He has so much potential as a lover that I cannot wait to recover my strength."

He shook his head at her brazen words and took his leave. Banks rushed past him to return to Felicity. Young love, or lust. Had he ever felt that way? He couldn't remember doing so but supposed he likely had at some time in the past.

His chamber was empty of Marinari but a cloth wrapped bundle lay hidden under his hat. Slowly, he unwrapped the gift and found a jar of oil and a small marble dildo in his palm. The thought of that cold marble and the obvious place he should put it made his heart pound with fear, lust, and anxiety. He had never tried one before, but the duke had a large collection and chose them personally for the club so Francis was aware they came in all sizes and thicknesses. This one was for a novice. Could he fit it himself?

He shook his head and stuffed both items deep in a drawer and closed it again. The duke did not want him that way and it was high time he set the matter from his mind. With his duties done here, he would return to his other patient and pretend those kisses from the morning had never happened, or that the duke had turned away so resolutely after.

He walked the long distance home, worry turning his stomach in knots over the chances of retaining his employment. He had no choice but to return to the duke's service, even if he had overstepped his position. He had nowhere else to go but home to his brother's house and backbreaking farm work.

The housekeeper smiled hesitantly as he passed through her domain. Usually the woman was happy to see him. Not so this afternoon, it seemed. It was very likely that the other servants had overheard him shouting at the duke and his son and would rightly be waiting for him to be dismissed from service.

The short climb to his chamber had never seemed so long. He slipped into his small room, locking the door behind him as he considered his options. But he couldn't think of any. He was the duke's man. Had been since age ten. What else was there to do aside from farming on his brother's land? His back ached at the thought of ending his life in manual labor, the very thing his father had been adamant he escape.

Francis slipped off his clothes—he stank of sweat and fear—and quickly ran a soapy washcloth over his skin before changing into the fresher, finer attire required to be worn in the duke's service. He had grown spoiled by his easier lifestyle. He didn't relish a change.

When he was ready, he headed for the duke's chamber

and, after a deep breath, tapped on the door.

"Get in here, Red," the duke called immediately.

He set his hand to the door and pushed it open. The duke still lay in his bed, almost as Francis had left him, but Lord Bracknell paced the room. Francis closed the door quietly and warily approached the pair, unsure of his reception.

The duke smiled. "How does the club go on today?"

"Very well." Francis didn't say anymore, even if he should report Miss Felicity's improvement. Such conversations were forbidden within Lord Bracknell's hearing. Bracknell wasn't allowed inside the club or to know what went on there. He skirted the duke's son, and checked the duke's appearance carefully. His eyes drooped as if he were weary, his skin was pale. His hands were curled into the sheets, however, and that indicated he was in some pain. Bracknell should have noticed this himself, but as usual, the duke's son only thought of himself.

After his earlier outburst, Francis held his tongue from asking him to leave so the duke might rest. He did not wish to be dismissed out of hand, at least until the duke was well again.

"Rupert knows about the club, Red. About all of it," the duke murmured, eyes lifting to stare at him.

Francis pressed his lips together over a curse. At least that explained why Lord Bracknell paced and the duke appeared anxious. But why today, of all days? The duke's son would prove difficult about it all and likely cause his father additional distress. It was the worst time possible for this conversation to have happened. The duke was too weak to make a good argument.

He peeked at Bracknell as he passed to fetch wine for the duke's pain. The man appeared completely rattled by the news his father ran the most decadent and corrupt pleasure house in London, even if larger society had no clue about the goings on there. Bracknell looked about to tear his hair out.

On his way back to the duke, Bracknell caught his arm in a tight grip. "I owe you an apology. I know you worked hard to save my father. I should not have questioned your loyalty to him or the family. Especially not now."

"None required." Francis shook off the grip and moved to the duke's side. A half-hearted apology at best, but still a surprise. He held the glass to the duke's lips. Staines lifted one hand and set his fingertips to the back of Francis' to steady the glass. After the conversation with Marinari, his heart pounded wildly at the contact.

The duke's head fell to the pillow, a tired smile twisting his lips. "Thank you for coming back."

He swallowed hard. "My place is here."

The duke's smile brightened. "It is. Red," he swallowed, "can you get me out of these damned clothes soon? I feel ridiculous lying here half-dressed."

CHAPTER EIGHT

Ambrose couldn't believe his eyes. Francis Redding was blushing at the thought of undressing him. He let out a relieved breath then quickly looked at his son. Rupert was still in shock about the club and the goings on that happened there behind closed doors, so he likely would not immediately notice the way his servant's trousers had swelled around his groin. He'd better convince Rupert to go away and soon. He had a lot to talk to his footman about he didn't want overheard before this damn headache grew worse.

He licked his lips. "Rupert. Could we continue this conversation tomorrow? I'm weary."

His son nodded absently, then he glanced up. "I want to see inside the club."

The flare of pain in his head made tonight an impossibility. He wasn't feeling well, although a lot better since Red had returned. How long would Rupert wait before taking the matter into his own hands? He glanced quickly at Francis.

His footman met his gaze. "You must rest for a few days, Your Grace. Any tour by you will have to wait at least a week before I'd advise venturing out for even a short trip."

A week? He winced. Rupert was an impatient man. He'd never wait that long before mounting an assault on the club. Ambrose shifted his left arm and bumped against Francis. "I cannot order this, but will you take him on a tour of the place early tomorrow. Sign him in first and introduce him to Marinari."

Francis frowned. "I can, unless Lord Bracknell disagrees and prefers to wait for you."

Relief coursed through him. It was cowardly, of course, but he had not wanted to walk into the club's torture room with his eldest son and explain about those who found their pleasure in chains. There were many things he had to keep secret from his son about his own sexual proclivities. A discussion of what he didn't like would surely lead to more questions about what he did like. Rupert would be like the rest of society, he'd be appalled his father made love to men as well as women.

"Tomorrow at ten?" Rupert asked.

Francis nodded. "As long as His Grace has rested well during the night, then I am at your disposal. Shall I meet you there?"

"No, here." Rupert took two paces toward the door and stopped. "Rest well, Father. I'll see you tomorrow."

When the door shut behind his son, Ambrose cursed aloud. "He called me Father again."

Francis shrugged and set a hand to Ambrose's brow. "I wouldn't worry about it right now. You're running a fever."

"I have a headache." Ambrose met Francis' gaze. "That isn't good, is it?"

Francis swallowed. "No, Your Grace. But it's early days yet. Let me get you comfortable again."

While his footman removed his clothing without a word, Ambrose worried. He'd thought when his mind was clear earlier that the injury could be behind him. An infection could kill him if it grew severe enough. He swallowed as a lump formed in his throat. He didn't want to die. Despite Francis' possible objection, he curled his good arm about his leg and squeezed. "Don't leave me again."

How pathetic he sounded, but he was terrified of dying and dying alone. He was terrified of losing Francis from his life. The man had always been on hand when he'd been injured, even when his late wife had been alive.

Francis ruffled his hair gently. "I'm here, Ambrose. Don't get into a fret. Let me check the wound again." He peered at the wound with a frown. "There is no infection forming that I can see." His lips pursed. "Perhaps you should rest now. I imagine the conversation with Lord Bracknell about the club was somewhat taxing on your strength. Perhaps that is the source of your headache."

He stroked Francis' wide thigh. "He did raise his voice a fair bit."

"I can imagine." His footman removed the hand from his leg, and when he did not release him immediately, Ambrose twined their fingers together. He had never been so relieved than when he'd heard Francis' customary knock on his bedchamber door. His heart had raced with impatience to touch him again.

He stroked his thumb over Francis' clenched fist and squeezed. "I take it I guessed correctly you had fled the house for the club. How is Miss Felicity getting on?"

Francis leaned against the bed, but didn't jostle him in the slightest. "Doing well. She has Mr. Banks dancing her tune, though. Caught them playing at cards in her chamber. All innocent, she assures me, but Banks could easily become infatuated with the woman."

"He told me last week he'd never fall in love," Ambrose chuckled. "I shall have to tease him if he should fall in love with her."

A rare smile crossed Francis' face and Ambrose tugged on their joined hands, urging him to sit on the bed. After a moment's hesitation, the man sat gingerly beside him, staring at where their joined hands now rested on his thigh. "Lust perhaps, but love?"

Ambrose stroked his skin again. "Stranger things have happened. It is impossible to decide whom you fall in love with."

His footman's face slacked of expression. Was he wondering about the possibilities of the pair of them as Ambrose was? His heart raced with excitement that Francis had not pulled away from him as yet. What more would the silent man allow?

Despite the pounding in his head, he wanted everything he could get and more. He wanted to kiss Francis again and this time he'd do a better job of it. He yearned for the other man's taste.

Very slowly, he brought their joined hands to his mouth. Francis followed the action, eyes wide, breath hitching, but he made no move to resist. Encouraged, Ambrose pressed light kisses to his knuckles, and then impulsively licked one.

The hand in his grip shook. "You should rest, Ambrose."

He turned Francis' hand palm up and pressed a kiss to the center. "I'll rest soon enough," he murmured against the rough skin.

Francis' fingertips scraped against his stubble. "This can wait 'till you're better, can't it?"

Ambrose grinned. "I'm impatient." He tugged Francis forward and kissed him fiercely, heart pounding as Francis kissed him back with as much passion. He threaded his fingers through coarse curled locks and held Francis close as he teased his tongue into his mouth, lighting little fires in his soul that he had no hope of dousing. He was alive again as he never had been. And the man returning his embrace was moaning softly into his mouth.

He grinned as he drew back. "I can wait 'till later, but not a second beyond that." A ruddy flush had swept over Francis' cheeks and he touched the clenched jaw reverently. "I'll get better soon."

When Francis set his head against Ambrose's, his breath a hard pant in the silent room, his heart pounded. He'd rattled his footman good and proper with his kisses. Pleased by that, he slid his hand down the other man's back to calm him. Heat radiated from the touch, making Ambrose realize that he was cold. He shivered.

Francis noticed, and quickly pulled the sheets and bedding higher around his shoulders. When he was done, he met Ambrose's gaze. "No more excitement, all right. You must rest if you want to be well again."

"I want it. I want you."

His footman smiled quickly, and then settled into the armchair. After a few minutes, he pulled the chair as close as possible and set his arm upon the bed so they touched. With that small sign of companionship, Ambrose closed his eyes and followed his orders.

While Ambrose thrashed on the bed in the grips of delirium, Francis hurriedly sponged him with a damp cloth. A high fever had developed during the night and he was afraid. Afraid that he'd missed a piece of linen, afraid the duke would die. But the wound showed no sign of infection and he was puzzled by the cause of the duke's restlessness.

He leaned close to the duke as morning approached and pressed his lips against the sleeping man's. The duke stilled in his dream and lifted his chin for more. Although it was a highly unlikely remedy for the affliction, the duke quieted after being thoroughly kissed, a discovery he'd made quite by accident. Francis slipped his tongue past the open lips and ravished the duke's willing mouth. When he stopped, the duke sighed with contentment and promptly fell asleep again.

That was the third time and Francis was starting to suspect the duke was doing it on purpose.

Weary beyond measure, Francis perched on the edge of the bed and considered lying down. He had to stay as close to the duke as possible, but he was so tired that he kept falling asleep where he sat. He slid sideways on the bed and rested his head on the empty pillow. The duke's fidgeting would surely wake him when necessary and he'd be up before anyone found him like this.

The duke moaned. Francis turned over quickly and peered at the duke's face in the gloom. His eyes were closed but he lifted his arm. "Come closer, Red. I won't bite. Yet. "

Surprise held him still a long moment then he shifted marginally closer. The duke hauled him against his good shoulder and settled Francis against his side. "Much better." Ambrose kissed the top his head. "I wondered what it would take to get you in my arms."

The duke sighed heavily and grew still again. Francis listened to the thudding heartbeat, regular as the tide, and knew exactly when he fell into a deep, healing sleep.

Yet Francis remained awake until the household stirred. Then as the rattle of pails echoed outside in the hall, he carefully extracted himself from the duke's bed to call for the duke's valet to relieve him while he took care of his own needs. He was starving and so should the duke be when he awoke.

Once Smith eventually arrived, he hurried down the servants' stairs to the kitchen and wolfed down the contents of the heaped plate set before him. By the time he was done, Cook had put together a new tray to tempt the duke's appetite. Everything the duke loved.

"A note came for you, Mr. Redding," Mrs. McClurry said from the doorway. When she held it out, Francis tucked it into his coat pocket to read later. He needed to get back to the duke. There was nothing more important.

Francis slipped into the chamber quietly in case the duke was still sleeping, but then he dropped the tray when he saw a man leaning over the duke's bed.

Ambrose jerked awake at the loud crash, groaning as his pleasant fantasy of making love to Redding by the riverbank ended suddenly. He blinked his eyes and swore. "Get the hell away from me."

Lord Silas jerked back. "It's only me."

His coy smile made his guts turn over. He glanced at the door where Francis stood immobile as a statue, and then he started backing out of the room. "Get your arse back in here, Red."

Lord Silas touched his bare leg where he'd escaped the sheets. "Send your servant away."

Silas skimmed his fingers gently up and down his skin, but Ambrose was anything but seduced. He shifted his leg and gestured for Francis to come closer. "Red, escort Lord Silas from the chamber. He is unwanted."

Francis' jaw worked furiously, but he didn't speak or move.

Ambrose frowned. "Damn it all." He rolled to his side with a groan and sat on the bed edge. Lord Silas shifted closer and before the young lord could touch him again he drew back his left arm and punched him in the jaw. He gasped as the impact shook his body and healing shoulder wound. "Is that clear enough for you? Get out."

Lord Silas stared up at him, gaze darting beyond them. "I know you have to pretend for the servants' benefit, but why did you have to hit so hard?" he whispered.

Ambrose shook his head at the obtuse man. "I don't want what you're offering. I told you I was otherwise engaged and I don't need some sniveling backdoorsman creeping into my sickroom. Get out. Don't come near me or my club again. Your membership is revoked and I have no wish to speak to you again."

"You cannot do that." Lord Silas drew himself up indignantly. "I know things about you that would ruin you and expose the club."

Ambrose stood suddenly, but a wave of dizziness swept him. Thankfully, Francis crossed the room and caught his elbow in a tight grip. He leaned on Francis and glared at Silas. "How long do you think you will live if you say one word about me or my club, eh? You signed the oath to keep the club's activities secret when you were admitted, just like every other member. Expose one, you expose everyone. Another member with less restraint than myself will likely kill you before you can blink. I wouldn't have to lift a finger to take my revenge if you should ruin us." Ambrose stared the man down, ignoring the ache in his shoulder as best he could. "Do we understand each other now, Lord Silas? Come at me and you come at every member of the club and will suffer the consequences."

Lord Silas ground his teeth, and then shot a look of venom at Francis. "So, you're the one," he hissed.

Francis blinked. "The one what?"

"The one he's chosen to be his next lover."

His footman dropped Ambrose's elbow and took a pace forward. "Say that again."

"You can't deny it. You're always watching him."

Instead of getting angry, Francis laughed. "Do you blame me? The duke might be a powerful man, but he has nothing except bad luck and accidents. My job, as the late duchess insisted, is to keep him out of harm's way. Would you like to see the handsome note she wrote before her death, asking me to keep him out of trouble? She didn't ask for much, our duchess, but she thought of her husband before herself. You got him shot by your jealous lover. I should beat you to a pulp for that fact alone."

Lord Silas lost some of his surety when Francis glared. He took a pace back. "I am not responsible for the duel or Fletcherly. I barely knew him."

Francis followed. "You first entertained Fletcherly at the Crow's Head Inn in Hatfield and spent an hour or two above stairs. Fletcherly is a very vocal man. He calls you 'sweetie', does he not?"

Silas gasped. "You cannot prove that."

Francis pivoted to face Ambrose. "Can I prove it, Your Grace? Do you remember the night last year when you stayed at the Crow's Head on your way to Lady Fairmont's first house party? When I returned with the brandy you requested, I was laughing."

Ambrose stumbled back to the bed and sat down wearily. "You wouldn't tell me the joke."

Francis raised one eyebrow. "Now you know." He turned back toward Silas. "While it would be my greatest wish to give you the thrashing you deserve for bringing harm to my employer I'm not going to hit you. As it is, you'll need that pretty face to snare your next bedfellow. You've nothing else to recommend you."

"I will not stand to be slandered by a mere servant and do nothing. You, sir, I shall see in court."

Ambrose laughed. "No, you won't. Redding, here, is the club's first member after myself. You cannot say a word against him, either."

Silas blustered, but Ambrose ignored him. Having Francis as a member was a stroke of devious planning on his part and he was grateful now that he'd not been dissuaded from setting that security in place. At the time, he'd said it was only to ensure the footman's silence and protect the club member's secrets, but it would also protect Redding as well.

Lord Silas stormed out, leaving the doors wide open behind him.

Francis pursed his lips and then strolled after him, stepping over the mess on the floor with barely a glance.

CHAPTER NINE

Francis closed and locked the doors to the duke's apartment. He rubbed a hand over the smooth surface, breathing hard as tension rose up to choke him. The duke had not denied he would be his next lover and, now that Silas had gone, he didn't know how to act. Behind him, the duke groaned loudly, the bed ropes creaking as he returned to bed.

He turned slowly to face the duke. His Grace had settled with every pillow piled behind his back, but his left hand covered his wound completely. Concerned, Francis stepped over the mess of broken china and crossed to the bed.

The sheets were pooled at Ambrose's waist, exposing the broad chest, flat stomach and trailing line of dark hair disappearing beneath. Francis swallowed, suddenly nervous and shy around the man he'd known all his life. The man he'd give his life for, if it was required. As if sensing his uncertainty, Ambrose held out his hand, palm up. Heart hammering, he covered it with his own and curled his fingers around the warm skin.

"I'll never understand men like Lord Silas," the duke whispered. "I never encouraged the fool. Let us hope he makes no more trouble."

Francis nodded, and the duke smiled. He tugged him closer until he sat on the bed edge.

"How long do you think before I am my old self? There is so much I want to do."

Ambrose lifted Francis' hand to his lips and the warmth of his mouth on skin had Francis gasping. "A few weeks, I imagine."

The duke opened his mouth wider and drew Francis' thumb into his mouth. He slowly sucked on the digit, stroking his flesh with his tongue. Francis panted. His cock thickened. When his thumb was released, Ambrose sat forward. They were eye to eye, both breathing roughly. "Can I anticipate being alone with you for those bothersome weeks?"

He licked his lips and Francis followed the movement. "If you want me, I'll be here. You're the duke."

"Oh, I want you. Right now, beneath me, and gasping for breath, but I fear I'm not capable of giving you complete satisfaction." Ambrose grinned suddenly. "Never thought I'd say that to anyone. Thank God you can keep a secret."

Francis nodded. "I keep many secrets." Mesmerized, he stroked the duke's chest with his fingertips, touching hard-pointed nipples and warm flesh. The duke closed his eyes, and Francis smoothed his palm down his ribs. "I'll always keep yours."

The duke opened his eyes. "And what of your secrets? Do I get to hear them, too? Do you want to leave my service and study as a physician?"

Now that he was touching Ambrose, Francis had a hard time following the conversation. He stroked his nipples again, catching the odd hitch to the duke's breathing, being caressed in return. As he lowered his head to taste the duke's flesh, Ambrose caught his chin and lifted his face.

Their eyes met. "Do you want to leave my service to become a physician?"

He frowned at the worry in his master's gaze. "No. But I would still like the freedom to study the lore, if I may."

"Of course you can." The touch to his chin grew into a caress. "But I need to dismiss you from my service, Francis. I cannot make love to a servant who is in my employ."

He drew away. "You would throw me out just because you desire me?"

Ambrose shook his head. "I have my rules, as you know. Seducing a servant goes against every principal I hold dear. I cannot make love to you as I wish to if you are here because you must be."

Francis raked his fingers through his hair. "I have had scores of lords approach me with offers of similar positions over the years. I turned them all down. I *am* here by choice, you idiot."

The duke shook his head. "It is not quite the same thing. I pay you a wage, put a roof over your head, and put food in your belly. You cannot say no to me."

The man had foolishness for brains. "You gave the duchess pin money, put a roof over her head, and gave her the best of everything. Are you saying she had no choice but to sleep in your bed? She loved you. Everyone knew that."

Ambrose dipped his head. Without a view of his face, Francis didn't know what he could be thinking. All he did know was that he was desperate to keep touching his skin. He leaned forward and set his lips to the duke's neck. The hot skin was smooth and warm and he nipped and licked across his left collarbone.

Ambrose embraced him with one arm. "Shall I treat you as a wife? Do you like diamonds or rubies?"

Francis lifted his lips for a bare moment. "Don't be an imbecile. Only sapphires will do." He pushed the duke gently back to his mound of pillows and kissed down his chest. He flicked his tongue over a tight nipple. Making love to a man was a new experience for him, but he still received the same whimpers of appreciation as from a woman, so he continued in the same vein.

Ambrose gasped. "Quite right. Quite right. Don't know what I was thinking. I'll open the vault as soon as you let me out of this bed."

Francis raised his head. "I was joking. I'm not at all like Marinari."

The duke ran his fingers over Francis' skull. "Thank God for that. She's an expensive minx. I'll buy you a new horse instead. We will be doing a lot of riding together when I'm healed." The duke grinned and kissed him fiercely. Angling his head for a deeper kiss, Francis swept his tongue deep into the duke's mouth with a hearty groan.

But doubts teased at the corners of his desire. Should he tell the duke he had never entertained a man before? As Ambrose pulled him atop his chest, he gathered his courage to make the confession. He hoped the duke did not laugh at his inexperience. He hoped he would not change his mind.

He hovered over the duke, keeping his weight from pressing on his wound and kissed him again. Kissing a man was different. There were gentle nips, the brush of whiskered jaw and taste of forbidden passion to stir his blood. He was harder than he'd ever been, groin pressed against the duke's obviously thick cock.

As if reading his mind, the duke worked his hand between them. Francis shuddered as strong fingers roughly closed over the aching bulge in his trousers. The touch turned gentle, and then the duke stretched to cup his balls. "Thought you'd be a handful," he groaned. "Cannot wait to get my mouth around you."

Francis shoved the hand aside and captured Ambrose. Without trousers or sheet between them now he had his first touch of another cock. Soft, silky skin like his, long, slightly thinner but just as hard. He looked down to where his hand shuttled over the hot flesh, groaning as he imagined the cock in his mouth or in his arse. That was going to be uncomfortable. He swallowed. "Ambrose," he started.

The duke covered his lips. "I promise to look after you. I'll take my time so you enjoy every minute in my bed, I swear. Trust me."

Francis stared into languorous eyes and nodded. "I trust you."

The duke wrapped his arm about Francis and squeezed. "Thank you."

Their lips met again, harder, hungrier and surer of their pleasure. Ambrose clutched Francis' bottom hard against him, caressing his cheek, slipping his fingers into the crack of his arse with more insistence. Francis groaned at the unfamiliar but arousing sensation.

He wanted everything the duke would do to him. He wanted it all now. He lifted up to tell Ambrose to take him this very instant, but a movement out of the corner of his eyes turned his head.

Lord Bracknell stood with the housekeeper's keys

swinging in his hand and murder plain in his eyes. Francis sat up, swiveling to face the bedchamber door.

The lord's son blinked. "What the devil are you doing to my father? I'll see you hanged for this."

CHAPTER TEN

Ambrose's lust drained away as if it had never been. Dear God, that boy of his had the worst timing. If he had just waited ten more minutes he would have never seen Francis' acceptance of their passion and both of them wouldn't have had hard cocks on display. He flicked the sheet over his hips. "Learn to knock."

"If I had knocked I wouldn't have caught him molesting you." Rupert hurried across the room toward Francis and swung a punch. Quick as lightning, Francis dumped his son on the floor and set a knee to his back.

"Release me, you damned sodomite," Rupert hissed.

"Keep him there, Red, while I find a robe." Slowly, Ambrose shuffled around the room, snatching a robe from a distant chair, locking the door and then struggling to get his arms into the sleeves. "Damn, that stings." He tied the belt slowly, and then approached his violently thrashing son. "Stand him up."

Francis hauled Rupert to his feet as if he weighed nothing. Although his son struggled, he couldn't free himself from Francis' hold.

He scowled. "Get this bastard off me."

"No. Francis does my bidding, not yours. You will listen to my explanation without interruption or I will make your life an absolute misery."

"How can you stand to be near him?"

"Very easily." He smiled. "Rupert, as you get better acquainted with the world you will discover that pleasure is found in many places. I happen to enjoy the company of men as well as women in my bed. Many do. Will you call me a damned sodomite, too?"

Rupert's mouth fell open. "You can't be serious."

Ambrose shook his head. "I pursued Redding. Not the other way around. He is a good and honorable man, Rupert. Loyal, completely devoted to me, and to our family. How could I not want the rest of him?"

"Why?"

Ambrose frowned. "The matter is none of your business. Just as your personal life, including who you take to your bed while you are married to Sally, is none of mine."

Rupert struggled. "It's unnatural."

From what he could see, Rupert did not understand his attraction and he didn't know how to convince him that there was nothing he wanted to change about his life, except maybe hurrying along his health so he could recommence seducing Francis.

He was about to speak when Francis leaned close to Rupert ear. "Do you remember Lord Ives, my lord?"

"We attended Eton together." Rupert paled and Ambrose drew closer. "What about him?"

"Such a sad case. They claimed his death an accident but, really, who shoots their cock off by mistake?"

"He never did," Rupert whispered, eyes widening in horror.

A look of profound sympathy crossed Francis' face. "I'm afraid he did. You know why, don't you?"

Rupert shook his head. "I know nothing about the matter. I heard it was an accident and that is the end of it."

Ambrose set his good hand to his hip. "Well, I'd like to know what the two of you are talking of. Francis, the details if you please."

Rupert looked about to faint.

Francis slowly released his hold and took a few steps back. "I'm afraid I cannot share them, Your Grace. The matter was laid to rest long ago. Trust me. You do not need to know the details. Everyone has secrets that should be kept. I'm sure his lordship will agree."

He considered insisting but something in the way Rupert stood, drained of fight and filled with sadness, stopped him from asking further. If Francis thought he didn't need to know then he would trust him to keep the knowledge to himself. He wouldn't reveal family secrets. He already knew so many. And the leverage of having a quiet hold over Rupert might help his son forget or ignore what he'd seen them doing in his bed because he had no intention of stopping.

"What did you come to see me about, Rupert?"

His son's head rose. "The doctor has confirmed my wife is with child. I thought you would be anxious to hear the news firsthand."

Ambrose beamed. "Congratulations." He stepped forward to embrace his son, but Rupert took a pace back suddenly. He frowned at his retreat.

"I should be going," Rupert mumbled, and then hurried for the door.

Ambrose watched him go, saddened that his boy would no longer look at him. It wasn't the worst scenario he'd imagined. But at least he still had his head.

Francis caught his hand and squeezed. "He'll come around; I've no doubt of that. Give him time."

He leaned against the one man who'd always accepted his nature as a normal one. "What do you know about him that I don't?"

Francis curled an arm around Ambrose's waist and shuffled him back toward the bed. "That he is as stubborn as his father and loves his family. Don't worry about him. Worry about you."

"Why? Am I in danger?"

Francis chuckled against his neck and pressed light kisses against his skin. "No danger to be found here, but—" he slid a hand between the folds of Ambrose's robe and stroked his cock "—you might worry if I'll ever let you come before I'm through."

Ambrose's pulse hammered. "Lock the door, Red, and put a chair under the handles, too, just in case Rupert comes back. I don't want any more interruptions today."

Francis nipped his neck. "Stay here." His lover left him suddenly, locked the door, jammed a chair beneath the knob and returned before his cock even felt the cold. Instead of tumbling him into bed, Francis tugged him toward the wall and pulled him hard against his groin. They kissed, tongues stumbling over each others in their rush to taste. Although his right shoulder ached, he did what he could to caress his lover with both hands.

His footman turned him suddenly, pressing his thick cock against his thinly covered arse. After a huff, he teased the silk robe from Ambrose's shoulders and the expensive garment pooled at their feet. He kicked it away as Francis captured his hips. He tugged, and Ambrose landed hard against bare, scorching skin. He gasped at the pleasure of the touch and tried to turn.

"Stay like this." Francis dipped and his thick cock slid between his thighs and nudged his bollocks with the hot tip. "Please," Francis whispered.

He captured Ambrose's cock with a heavy groan and he shuffled his hand over the aching length. When he worked his member back and forth beneath Ambrose's body, Ambrose shook.

"God, that feels good." He turned his head, and met his lover's lust filled eyes. "Why did I wait so long?"

"Because you are an idiot, Your Grace." Francis kissed him swiftly. "But a sick one, so I will do all the work. You like this?"

"Hell, what's not to like," he whispered, taking care to keep from shouting his pleasure loud for the whole house to hear. "The only thing better would be if you fucked me with that monster."

"I didn't think."

"Oh, I do. I like to give and receive. In fact, stick your hand into that drawer. Top drawer, near the back."

His cock was released and the small bottle of oil extracted. But Francis frowned. "What is this for?"

"My arse and your cock. We'll need some lubrication for a comfortable fit."

"Oh."

He smiled at Francis' expression and worked the stopper from the bottle. "Rub some on your length and some on my arse then line up and take me. I'm yours if you want me."

A silly grin crossed Francis' face as he quickly applied the oil, but when his hand rose, glistening with the slick substance, he looked confused. Ambrose grabbed his wrist and thrust his hand against his own arse. Slowly, he probed between his cheeks and he almost spilled his seed at the first touch. Hell, he might not last a minute beyond being taken. The thought of Francis sliding inside him made him quiver.

He took a deep breath to steady himself, and then leaned against the wall. He pulled one cheek aside. Warmth crowded his back, warm hands touching him intimately. And then the large head pressed against him. Unfortunately, the alignment wasn't perfect. Ambrose captured the slick length and guided Francis slightly lower.

He grunted when his hole stretched, kept his breathing slow and calm as Francis claimed him. He folded his arm on the wall at the wonder of the incredible sensation. A slight pinching burned his ring as Francis slowly worked himself deeper. When he was settled deep, Ambrose opened his eyes and glanced over his shoulder.

"Oh, fuck," Francis groaned. He began to thrust and it was heavenly. Making love to the right man made all the difference.

He pushed back against his lover, encouraging him to a rougher taking. Francis tightened his fingers on his hips, grinding them together relentlessly as pleasure took them closer to the abyss.

Ambrose glanced down at his aching cock, watching it bob with each hard thrust and leak more seed. He set his head to the wall so he could stroke his flesh, but as his fingers curled around his length, Francis' oily palm covered them.

"Allow me," his lover whispered against his ear, his movements slowing to a snail's pace. The slide of an oiled hand, the sense of anticipation fizzling along his nerves, brought Ambrose close to the brink.

He nodded since his shoulder ached like fire, but wished he wasn't so useless.

He pressed his arm to the wall as Francis stroked his flesh, fucked his arse harder, and reveled in his lover's softly uttered grunts. His bollocks drew up tight, arse stinging as Francis grew frenzied and when his lover groaned into his hair he came, spurting his release against the wall with a satisfying splat.

He shook from the force of it. From the strength of emotion behind the pleasure. It had been so long since he'd felt connected beyond physical satisfaction so he reached for his lover's leg to keep them connected as long as possible. After a time, Francis slipped free of him. The loss of that thick length made him want it all over again. He turned around and leaned against the wall for support.

Francis crowded him. "Is your shoulder all right?"

So considerate. Ambrose chuckled softly. He looped his good arm over the broad shoulder and drew Francis' head closer for a kiss. "Of course I'm all right. I have you."

CHAPTER ELEVEN

Sitting alone in a carriage with Lord Bracknell the day after being found kissing his father was perhaps not the safest activity Francis had ever engaged in. Bracknell was sullen, spoke only in clipped tones, and stared out the carriage window as they rumbled along London's streets. But Bracknell had offered him a seat inside the carriage, rather than atop beside the grooms getting drenched in the rain, so he did his best to be unobtrusive and give him no cause to be more annoyed.

As the carriage pulled up at the rear of the building, Francis stepped out first, waved away the groom and held the door open.

Bracknell joined him, but he was scowling. "Why the rear entrance?"

"His Grace's orders, my lord. He wanted you to see everything else before the patrons know you are admitted to the club." He leaned a little closer so the grooms would not overhear. "Since you have no idea what goes on, and society is aware you are not a member, you can greet everyone later with all the facts in your possession. His Grace did not want you to be uncomfortable."

Bracknell strode forward. "And he didn't think that would already have been the case? I've had dozens of lords laughing at my ignorance for years."

Francis gritted his teeth. He'd known of the jibes aimed at Bracknell. It was his job to protect the family, but he hadn't stepped in often enough, it seemed. Perhaps that accounted for Bracknell's perpetual bad mood.

He ushered the duke's son inside and led him to the small anteroom's desk and saw the membership register had been moved here as he had requested. "If you could just sign the register, my lord, we can then proceed upstairs."

Bracknell's jaw clenched.

He sighed. "No one is allowed beyond this chamber without signing."

When Bracknell remained still, Francis flipped the pages to the first and pointed at the duke's name, his own name, the duke's of Byworth and Lewes. The very first club members.

Bracknell's jaw loosened and he signed his name with a flourish.

Francis snapped the book shut and shoved it under his arm. "There are twenty-three rooms within the house. The great room and gallery, dining room and library on the lower levels, but above stairs is where the club differs from most others. Here a lord can find pleasure of every sort imaginable, and some I don't understand at all." He pointed along a narrow corridor. "Patrons come through there from the front rooms and into this reception chamber."

Bracknell nodded, gaze sweeping over what he could see from floor to ceiling.

At this hour, the whores were still preparing for the coming night, but he would have to assemble them for Bracknell's perusal later.

The movement of red silk across the chamber drew his attention. Of course Marinari would be keen to make the acquaintance of the club's new lord and master. What he hadn't worked out was whether Bracknell would realize that she was a man beneath the fine silks or if he'd have to tell him.

"Redding, so good to see you, darling. Who is this fine gentleman? I must make his acquaintance."

Francis rolled his eyes as Bracknell dipped his head. Marinari knew exactly who he was, the minx. But he performed the introductions, wincing when Bracknell behaved as if he spoke to a woman. He'd have to tell him then.

Marinari slipped her arm through Bracknell's. "So, you have come to us at last. I had begun to fear the duke would never relent and keep you from us indefinitely. We are, of course, at your complete disposal."

"Thank you," Bracknell murmured.

"Marinari, remember the duke's rules."

She turned. "Every rule can be broken."

An uncomfortable flush swept his skin. Bracknell scowled and Marinari laughed at him then began the tour with Bracknell on her arm. Instead of Francis being burdened with the chore, she did all the talking, sweeping the man from room to room, flirting with him shamelessly in the process. Bracknell lapped up the attention, nodded politely to the ladies when they presented themselves for his inspection. But he frowned at the growing number of men he encountered.

"Marinari, would you excuse us?"

Her smile faltered, but she did as Francis asked. He drew Bracknell into the next chamber and closed the door. "The club caters to many tastes, my lord. There are an equal number of ladies and fellows available in the club for pleasure."

"Was my surprise that obvious?" Bracknell grumbled. He crossed the room, pulled open a wardrobe and scanned the contents.

"I'm afraid so. There is worse to come. I didn't feel right not warning you."

A frown creased Bracknell's brow. "I always wondered why my father kept you around so much. Seems he couldn't risk letting you go. The things you could say, heh?" He swallowed. "Redding, why are the ladies' slippers so large?"

Francis peered around his shoulder and shrugged. "Those clothes do not belong to the whores here. They are garments and fripperies for the members to slip on if they enjoy them."

Bracknell slammed the doors closed. "I'm in a mad house."

"One can grow accustomed to madness."

"What exactly is your position with my father?" Bracknell turned. "You are certainly more than mere footman."

Disquiet rumbled through him. What exactly was he now? He didn't rightly know. "I joined the duke's household at age ten. Your grandsire preferred him to be always attended by servants, so I was added to their number to provide companionship while he prowled the estate."

Bracknell nodded, settling against the robe as if he'd forgotten the contents existed.

"Over time, when he'd grown more sure of himself and stood up to his family's strictures, your father dismissed the others and kept me exclusively."

Bracknell frowned. "I have a vague memory of you, from when I was a boy, standing behind my father in the driving rain beside my mother's grave not long after she was laid to rest."

He swallowed over the painful memory. "He grieved for her more than you know."

"Is that why he sent me away? Why I didn't see him for almost a year."

Francis raked his hand through his hair. He didn't like to speak of the duke this way and certainly not here where anyone could overhear them. He shouldn't say another word. "There is much more to see, my lord, if you would just come this way."

For the first time ever in Francis' memory, Bracknell let a subject drop without question. He followed him into the torture room and stopped dead still. Knowing it would take a while to process the contraptions in the room, Francis closed the door and leaned against the wall to wait. "Everything is cleaned and oiled daily. You may touch anything you're curious about."

Bracknell gave a nervous laugh but slowly circled the room, turning several dials on one particular device. His eyes widened impossibly. Most people behaved the same but not many returned for personal application to their body. While Bracknell rattled about, Francis relaxed, dropping his gaze to the floor. During the course of the morning, the other man had grown less surly toward him and that could only be for the good. He had winced when Bracknell avoided his father's touch yesterday and hoped he would not distance himself from his father's love. Ambrose would be unhappy.

Bracknell cleared his throat. "How many of the members would use this chamber?"

"Quite a few." He lifted his gaze to Bracknell. "More than half. But that wasn't your real question, was it?"

He shook his head.

Francis smiled as reassuringly as he could. "Your father has never used this chamber to my knowledge, or sought the entertainment among those he employs here. He has found his pleasures elsewhere since the club began. He's said more than once that a landlord should not piss in his own parlor, so to speak, unless he wanted trouble. The place is an investment to him. One he takes great pains to manage well. The whores are clean and biddable, violence is frowned upon, and those working here are paid a decent wage with adequate comforts for their labors. He would want that to continue."

"He doesn't dabble here because he has you?" Bracknell approached.

"He prefers gentlemen and ladies of his own rank."

Bracknell goggled. "At the same time?"

Francis bit his tongue. He should not have said a further word about the duke's adventurous sex life.

Suddenly, Bracknell laughed. "I have to hand it to my father. He certainly keeps his secrets well and truly hidden. I find I am amazed you've put up with him for so long, Red." Then he slapped his shoulder and stepped out into the hall.

Francis stilled in shock. A friendly slap, the shortening of his last name, didn't mean Bracknell had accepted his father's habits, but it did mean he wasn't quite so angry about yesterdays kiss. He drew in a deep breath and hurried from the room to finish the tour. Unfortunately, he couldn't see Bracknell anywhere in the hall.

He retraced his steps as far as the anteroom and when he still hadn't found Bracknell, he searched through the private parts of the club again.

An explosion of sound erupted down the hall and Bracknell burst into view, disheveled, panting and wide eyed. He was also rubbing his wrist in an alarming way.

Francis hurried to him as he spoke.

"She's a bloody man."

"Oh hell." He winced. "There was one more matter, my lord." Since Bracknell shook his hand so violently and wriggled his fingers without grimacing in pain, Francis concluded Marinari hadn't done more than enforce her opinion that she wasn't to be pawed at by a patron.

Bracknell scowled as she sauntered out the door with a wicked grin, hair perfect and a definite strut in her stride. "That," he growled, "I needed to know about, Redding." He covered his face with his hands then looked at them with horror. "He has a—"

Poor bastard. It was the first time Francis could ever remember feeling sorry for the duke's son. But it was also incredibly amusing. He wished Ambrose could have been here to see it. "I'd always assumed she was regularly proportioned but never considered satisfying my curiosity."

Bracknell's gaze pinned him in place. "Does my father know about him?"

Francis grinned in memory of that first introduction between Marinari and the duke. "You're quicker than your father. It took him a whole day of Marinari's flirting before he found out. I must say, your reactions are remarkably similar."

"Then why did he hire him if he was appalled?"

"Oh, he wasn't appalled. He was put out I figured it out first. You know how he is." He grinned. "Your father has a very open mind about what constitutes a man's acceptable pleasure. And he found a perfect bodyguard and bawd in the process. No one crosses Marinari."

Bracknell rubbed his wrist again.

"Did she injure you, my lord?"

"Of course not." He paused a long moment then shrugged. "She's only a woman."

Francis laughed at Bracknell's bravery in the face of certain disaster. Did he really not see the risk Marinari presented? "Marinari is as dangerous as a real one. Be cautious, my lord."

CHAPTER TWELVE

Ambrose impatiently paced his chamber. He was feeling remarkably good this morning, but he would feel so much better when Francis returned with his son. The club could be a permanent wedge between them, if Rupert allowed it to be.

China rattled behind him as Smith set out the luncheon tray. "Is there anything else you desire, Your Grace?"

He winced at the pleading edge to his valet's words. Francis was right again, the man did spend an inordinate amount of time eyeing his private parts. Damned uncomfortable morning since he'd need assistance donning every article he wore. "No, nothing, Smith. You may go. I'll not need you this evening."

There was some more fussing behind him then the room grew quiet. When he turned he found a small flower on his tray. He shuddered and tossed it into the fire. He much preferred his footman's quiet ways to fussing. He picked up a sandwich and returned to the window. Despite the dreary weather, London was awhirl with activity without him and for a change he didn't miss a bit of it.

When he thought about it, he mostly enjoyed his evenings out if Francis was with him and appeared amused by the event. The way he would press his lips together to hold in his laughter would fool everyone else, but Ambrose had always detected the spark of merriment in his eyes and played up until he frowned.

Now that he had Francis in his bed, he no longer felt restless except to see him return. Would society events become a crashing bore and a hindrance to enjoying his life fully? Quite possibly. He would have to find ways to be completely alone more often with Francis. But while his injury had allowed his footman to be by his side constantly these last days, they had to part at night. In Town, in the close confines of this house, Francis' comings and goings late at night would be noted by the other servants.

His valet would particularly notice the rumpled state of his bed should Francis spend the night in it. Talk would spread fast and that was an unacceptable risk to both of their lives. He'd have to be very cautious about how he conducted this affair. His mouth turned down at the thought. He didn't feel like he was engaged in an affair with a temporary lover. This, whatever it was with Francis, felt fated to be.

A timid knock sounded on the door.

"Come."

The door creaked open and his butler stepped into the room. "Everything is ready, Your Grace."

He rubbed his hands together and then winced at the pull on his newly healing skin. "Thank cook for arranging the dinner so quickly. You may bring up the dishes at seven and leave the clearing up 'till tomorrow. But make sure the footmen are unobserved when they come up. I want my dinner to be a surprise for Redding in thanks for all of his hard work."

An extravagant meal was a poor excuse for a thank you, but it was the best he could manage at short notice without leaving the house. He strolled to the adjoining chamber, impressed by the alterations that had taken place in the last two hours. The little used bedchamber made a perfectly acceptable small dining room. Since Francis would insist he rest often, he saw little point in traipsing up and down the staircase just for meals. Until he recovered his whole health, he would dine here and not in his bed. He refused to be treated as an invalid.

And today, Francis would dine with him.

He closed the door behind him a touch wearily and returned to his chamber. The bed was freshly made so he took the chair closest to the fire and picked up an open book. He frowned at the sketches as he flipped the pages. The book must be Francis' because he'd never want to read about the subject. Curing the mad and diseased didn't interest him, but apparently his lover had a curious mind.

Perhaps he could turn his thoughts toward ways to increase their pleasure. His cock thickened at the thought.

"Are you unable to rest, Your Grace?"

Ambrose looked up and grinned. "I was bored, Red."

"Not an unusual statement." Francis closed the door with a sharp snap and crossed the chamber. "You must rest."

"I will later. How did it go?"

"Better than expected. He was fairly surprised but not offended in any part. I introduced him to Marinari as you requested."

"I thought those two would get along famously."

Francis settled beside him. "Well, I don't know about famously, but I doubt their meeting will be one either will forget." Francis grinned suddenly. "Your boy found out the hard way what Marinari hides beneath her gown."

Ambrose groaned. "I should have been there."

Francis nodded solemnly. "I wish you had been." He raised an eyebrow. "It was so damned funny I couldn't believe you missed it."

He smiled at his lover's gentle chiding. That was what he liked about Francis. Every now and then he forgot he spoke to a duke and let down his guard. Very few people did that. He set a hand to Francis' thigh. "Come on, out with it. I want all the scandalous details."

The light in his lover's eyes brightened as he related the state he'd found Rupert, rumpled and horrified at where his hand had been. They laughed quietly over his shock while Ambrose gently rubbed the warm thigh under his hand. He dipped his gaze to Francis' groin and noticed the flattering bulge. He turned sideways and slid his hand over it. A rough gasp passed Francis' lips.

He worked the buttons free, opened his trousers. The thick cock sprang out as if desperate for attention. More than happy to oblige, he stroked the smooth, papery soft flesh, then wrapped his hand around the hot length. He moved, sliding his hand far down the shaft then back up to the tip before repeating the maneuver.

He wanted to taste but had an idea his shoulder would protest if he bent that far. He'd have to have Francis straddle his thighs if he wanted that monster in his mouth. The idea was simply too appealing to ignore. He sat back. "Come sit over me."

Francis frowned at his request. Ambrose tugged on the cock in his hand and encouraging Francis to move. Eventually, he got his lover where he wanted him, knees planted on either side of his thighs, trousers lowered, and his cock level with his chest. He put his hand to Francis' bare rear and pulled him up. His hot length nudged his cheek and he turned his head to suck on the tip.

Above him, Francis let out a shuddering breath and cupped his head.

His mouth watered, so he lapped the length generously, and then opened his mouth wider. The pleasant taste of seed coated his tongue and he sucked the salty flavor down quickly, hungry for more. He slowly bobbed his head but his shoulder ached even from that little movement.

But he wouldn't end this because of the pain. He dug his fingers into the full orbs beneath his hands and encouraged Red to move his hips. Francis thrust slowly, working his cock past his lips, gently doing his best not to force too much in at once. When they found an easy depth for him to manage, Ambrose wriggled his fingers between Francis' cheeks and stoked over his hole.

Francis jerked, pushing his cock against the back of his throat. Ambrose adjusted quickly and was more careful not to surprise his lover. But that tight hole tempted him. Teasingly he pressed against its soft pucker, again and again. He withdrew his hand, slipped the digit in beside the cock in his mouth and then returned to play.

"Now I don't wonder why you are so popular. The things you do, Ambrose."

He couldn't grin or respond and not lose the heavy flesh in his mouth, so he redoubled his attention to

Francis' arse. He found the center and pressed in a touch. The tight band of muscles resisted then gave a little and clamped around his finger. Francis grunted, his thrusts coming faster and harder at the sensations. Ambrose quickly swallowed and wriggled his finger.

Francis' grunts turned to louder groans and then he stilled, shuddering, coating Ambrose's tongue with his seed. Ambrose swallowed quickly then licked the cock before him clean and pressed a kiss to the slit. But his own cock ached with unreleased tension.

Francis dropped to the floor and knelt between his knees. He roughly jerked Ambrose's trousers open and lowered his head.

He hissed at the fevered attention, the warm, wet mouth enclosing him, and the fact that it was Francis devouring him. He shifted a little to see his cock being swallowed, but the awkwardness of his lover's movements excited him too much to watch for long. He closed his eyes. He wouldn't last beyond a moment. He, a man who could go all night if he desired it, was coming undone at the simplest pleasures.

And then Francis sucked hard. His balls drew up tight, he threaded his fingers into Francis' hair hoping to hold off, but before too long he shot seed straight down his lover's throat. Francis gagged in surprise but then swallowed, and lapped ravenously at his cock.

After a while, Ambrose nudged him back. "Do you do everything well the first time, Francis?"

"I don't know. I haven't tried everything yet."

His cheeky grin made Ambrose's heart flutter and he leaned forward to capture his lips rather than voice the words that had almost tumbled out. It was far too soon to confess he was in love, but he very much feared he felt as much for his servant as he had for his late wife. A strange and comforting thought. Francis would never replace Anna. It was a different sort of affection. But both his wife and oldest friend were equally important to him.

He embraced his lover quickly. How long could he hide his feelings?

CHAPTER THIRTEEN

It was late by the time Francis returned to his bedchamber, just after the clocks had struck four in the morning. He'd enjoyed the surprise thank you dinner, even if one wasn't necessary and he'd stayed with Ambrose until he'd fallen asleep, all the while keeping a discreet watch for signs of a relapse. But his lover's sleep was deep, sated, and he'd barely twitched as Francis had crept from the room.

It was strange to think of Ambrose as his lover. Harder still to believe they were so comfortable with the change. There was that small spark of shared awareness when they would look at each other, and without words, correctly guess what the other was thinking or about to do. And there was trust.

He sank onto his bed and stretched out his legs. He wriggled to get comfortable, noticing every lump beneath the rough blankets. Not like the duke's bed at all. Ambrose slept in luxurious comfort. He sighed at the memory of curling up beside him as he had last night. One of the best nights of his life, even if he hadn't slept a wink. He hadn't known the duke was fond of cuddling his lovers, or touching them as much as he did. Francis frowned. He couldn't ever remember seeing Ambrose touch a lover except to kiss her fingers or shake a gloved hand swiftly in greeting.

Well, there was the late duchess. Her Grace had been a tactile person and the duke had followed her around within the house like a faithful puppy. Perhaps that was unkind, but Ambrose did tend to pant when he was aroused and the duchess had known exactly what to do to keep him coming back, even when her mood turned blue. He hadn't liked her to travel alone either, so they had spent almost all of the decade-long marriage side by side. Francis put a hand over his eyes. How long could he keep the duke content before he was replaced?

Would Ambrose be content enough with only him for pleasure while his injury healed? Would he return to the *ton* in triumph and find someone else as soon as he was well?

Neither thought came with an answer. Ambrose had never kept a lover for long, except perhaps the Duke of Byworth. But that had been long ago, before either of them had married and their responsibilities had overwhelmed them. If the odds played out true to form, at least Francis could be assured Ambrose would not dismiss him when the affair ended. The duke remained on good terms with all his previous lovers, perhaps because he only made love to friends.

At least that was something. Ambrose didn't choose bed partners lightly. He chose lovers who had an open mind about when the affair would end.

That wasn't him. Francis had known the minute Ambrose had allowed him to fuck him that he'd found the place he belonged. He was the duke's man, body and soul. Even Ambrose had teased that he'd become his new wife in all but gender. He did tend to fuss and worry about the duke a great deal. Now they were lovers, he doubted he'd be able to stop. He'd probably worry more than he did in the past and that could prove a sticking point for the duke.

He liked his freedom.

He liked to come and go at his own whim.

Francis rolled to his side and stared across the narrow chamber at his precious books, the sum total of his wealth and consequence. He didn't amount to much, but everything he had and was belonged to the duke. Not much of a dowry. He laughed at the thought, amazed he imagined himself as the duke's new spouse. For one thing, the duke could never visit him in bed here, and another, he wouldn't want to visit this shabby chamber.

That kind of companionship wasn't possible for him. He would have nothing more than quick tumbles and his regular routine.

He set a hand to his chest at the uncomfortable life

ahead of him when the duke had had his fill. But paper crackled within his coat pocket and he sat up to remove it, squinting at the letters in the weak light. He couldn't see very much, so he stood and moved closer to the candle he hadn't yet blown out. His breath ceased as he recognized the handwriting. Why on earth was his brother's wife writing to him? Fanny didn't like to bother him when he was in London.

He ripped the note open and quickly scanned the close written sheet.

"Dear God." His legs buckled and he sank into a chair. His brother had been trapped under a fallen horse by the old stream. He squeezed his eyes shut as fear overwhelmed him. His brother was likely dead by now. Few men survived that kind of injury. He read the note again, taking more time to consider his brother's chances. A surgeon had attended him, and he was supposed to be resting comfortably in bed. Fanny had thought he would want to know.

Guilt tore at him.

If he'd been with his family he would be certain of Albert's chances of recovery or not. It may not be as bad as he had first feared. It might be far worse. Indecision gripped him but one thing was certain—he needed to return home and see for himself. Perhaps he could be useful to his brother and wife around the farm. Even if Albert recovered, he might never walk surely again.

He quickly gathered up the bare essentials he would take with him—surgeon's tools, clothes and coin—and then lay back down to impatiently wait for sunrise. At this hour, he'd be the only one awake and he could not leave the duke's side without explaining why he had to go. He'd need a horse or to take the public coach. He squeezed his eyes shut, but bloodied images of his brother tormented him. He sat up suddenly to expel them.

Sleep would likely not come to him this night, so he dressed himself in fresh clothing, set his belongings near the door, and quietly padded back toward the duke's chamber. The duke still slept and, as he stared down at the sleeping man his heartbeat doubled. What kind of mischief could he get into while he was gone? Would Lord Silas return and attempt to seduce him again? Would someone else replace him before he'd been gone a day? His stomach turned over at the thought.

"Come to bed, Francis," Ambrose murmured, pushing the sheets away from his side.

Although he should be cautious about being in the duke's bed, he slipped off his boots and lay down. The thought of resting his head on the duke's shoulder one last time was too tempting to ignore.

The duke shifted, and then flopped on top of him. "Mmm, that's what was missing. My new wife." Ambrose kissed his chest, and then stilled.

Cautiously, Francis curled his arms about the naked duke and listened to his breathing as he settled. He could get to like laying in this bed more than was good for him. Impulsively, he kissed the duke's hair. He would miss him while he was gone.

Ambrose stirred. "What's the matter, Francis?"

He swallowed. This wasn't quite the place he'd wanted to have the conversation about leaving, but he supposed no time would be pleasant. "I have to go home."

"When the Season is over we will return to Tindel Park." Ambrose slipped his hand under Francis' waistcoat and squeezed.

"No, now. I have to leave today."

The duke stilled. "Why the rush to get away from London? Are you unhappy with our new arrangement?"

Francis sighed and rubbed Ambrose's bare back. "My brother has been injured. I want to see that the right things have been done for him. And Fanny will need me about."

"Especially with Molly's coming out so close," the duke murmured. "Someone has to keep a good eye on that minx before she gets into serious trouble. Your brother had been doing an admirable job of it until now. But she's at *that* age. The adventurous one."

He squirmed to see the duke's face. His eyes were still closed, but his lips had lifted into a contented smile.

"Did you think I didn't listen when you spoke of your

family?" Ambrose squeezed his chest. "I know how important they are to you. We will go home today."

"There is no need to come with me. You should stay here and regain your strength before a long journey."

"There is every need. I won't be left behind wondering what is going on. Give Angus the word we want to close Tindel House for the rest of the Season. We'll go home after we get some more sleep this morning." Ambrose snuggled closer. "Don't argue. You'll only worry about what I'm up to here and become surly with Fanny and her nattering. You can visit her and have a reliable excuse to return home at night. Your nephews are not complete imbeciles. They can be relied upon to do some of the watching, too. Much better this way, don't you think?"

Francis let out the breath he had unwittingly held, stunned beyond words the duke was determined to upend his plans for the Season and return home just because Francis needed to go. He'd thought Ambrose asked questions about his family only to be polite, but it seemed as if he'd been more interested than he let on.

Would he ever understand what made him tick?

Ambrose rolled off him suddenly, grumbling a bit about his shoulder then fell straight back to sleep. Francis peered at him in the weak light. The duke kept himself fit, his skin tanned from swimming half-naked in his river when at home. Hesitantly, he set a hand over the broad chest and marveled that he was allowed to touch him. He withdrew his hand, lest he wake Ambrose again, but his heartbeat sped up at the idea that he was wanted for more than just immediate pleasure. That this affair between them could become something far more.

Weariness tugged at Francis' eyes, but he couldn't risk falling asleep in the duke's bed. He couldn't risk being found this way by the duke's valet. The man would likely have a fit of the vapors because it wasn't him there. He crept off the mattress, sat on a nearby chair and pulled on his boots. He'd sleep here beside the bed, ensure the duke was well enough to travel when he woke, and then make all the necessary plans to shift the duke home to Tindel Park.

CHAPTER FOURTEEN

"You sent for me, Father?"

Ambrose studied his reflection in the mirror one last time and then slowly turned. Fast movements still caused him discomfort, as he'd discovered while attempting to dress himself this morning without his valet's assistance.

"Morning, Ru. Thank you for coming so promptly." He assessed his son. Rupert appeared at ease today, if not exactly affectionate. He stood a few feet further away than was usual. "I thought I should inform you in person I'm returning to Tindel Park this morning."

Rupert took a step forward and clasped Ambrose's good arm. "Are you well enough to make the trip?"

A lump formed in his throat. At least he hadn't lost his son entirely with the revelations of the past few days. He nodded. "I'm leaving you in charge of the Hunt Club as of today. Rely upon Marinari as I have relied upon Redding and you will have no trouble running the place."

Rupert scowled. "Rely on that effeminate molly? Surely you must be joking."

"Marinari is more cunning than you give her credit for, and a great deal stronger."

Rupert crossed his arms over his chest. "I doubt that."

"One of these days, my boy, you will listen to your old father. Marinari is capable of keeping the unwise in line and ensuring the private aspects of the club run smoothly."

"I cannot imagine why I would need that man."

"Woman," Ambrose corrected. "These are troubled times, Rupert. Marinari has been living in this country in disguise for the past six years, five of them under my roof. I have never had cause to doubt her change of allegiance and I would appreciate it if you did not expose that."

"Why does he need to remain hidden?"

"Marinari was an assassin." Ambrose shuddered. "As Redding discovered after some careful digging, her family was slaughtered by the French in retaliation for an assignment gone wrong. Marinari was blameless, but they were killed, from her aged grandmother down to the smallest babe. Not one member of the family remains."

Rupert gasped. "Father, I know you have a soft spot for those beneath you, but this is taking it too far. You put our family in danger. If the Crown finds out—"

"Those who need to know are well aware of Marinari's location. She is being watched by many concerned parties."

"And you trust them to know of the club's goings on? You really are mad."

Ambrose grinned. "Those particular fellows were members long before Marinari came along. Don't fret about them. They will reveal themselves to you when they get to know your character better."

His son scowled. "I've never heard a whisper of a famous spy by the name of Marinari."

Ambrose shrugged. "Of course not. He changed his name, too, and keeps a low profile."

"So, who is he really?"

He supposed it unfair to leave his heir oblivious to the danger he faced should he be inclined to delve under Marinari's skirts again. The next time he may not get off so lightly. However, he had given his word. "You will have to wait for Marinari to trust you to learn that."

A tap sounded on the door and Smith hurried in and through the room at his summons. He rushed out again with his arms full and an unhappy scowl for his employer. Smith had to be dismissed.

"So, you really are going. But why the rush?"

"It is necessary. However, I wonder if you might do me a favor and take Smith into your household. He's poorly suited to country life."

Rupert raised an eyebrow. "Of course. My brother-in-law is with us and could use his own man rather than sharing mine. Have him sent 'round tomorrow." Rupert looked about him. "It will be very quiet in London without you this Season. You've always been here when I have been."

"I shall leave tantalizing the ladies of society in your capable hands." Ambrose laughed. "Just remember, if my absence grows too harsh to bear you can always visit us at Tindel Park. I should like to see you and Sally at Christmas."

"You're going to be gone that long?"

The door opened silently and Redding stepped inside the bedchamber.

Ambrose smiled quickly. He was trying his best to hide how terrible he felt before Francis so he wouldn't refuse him this trip. He couldn't allow the man to leave without him, not when their relationship was so new. What if distance and time apart convinced Francis an affair with him was a bad idea?

He needed the time and privacy afforded by Tindel Park to turn this into something lasting. If Francis had been a woman, they would already be bound for the border for an anvil wedding. As it was, he'd have to settle for a clandestine alliance. He returned his gaze to Rupert. "I'll make Tindel Park my permanent residence, I imagine. Society has lost its allure but I will be back should you need me."

Rupert swiveled slowly, spotted Francis waiting uncomfortably, and turned back. "Ah. Then I shall leave you in capable hands." He struck out a hand. "Safe journey, Papa."

"Be well, Rupert. My best to Sally."

⟡

Francis smiled as Bracknell embraced his father. He had worried that the breach between them would not be sealed before Ambrose departed London, but it seemed his worries had come to naught. He nodded as Bracknell stopped at his side.

"I hope you know what a bad bargain you're getting." He looked over his shoulder. "He's a handful."

He struggled to keep his amusement hidden at the dirty thought that popped into his head. He quite liked handling the duke's cock, but he couldn't very well tell Lord Bracknell. "I'll do my best to keep him out of trouble, my lord."

"I have no doubts you will." Bracknell slapped his shoulder good-naturedly and strolled out.

Once the door was closed again, Francis sauntered across the room. "Do I have any chance of convincing you not to make this trip?"

Ambrose grinned. "None whatsoever. I feel wonderful."

The duke didn't lie very well. He was still in pain judging by the look on his face. Francis shook his head. "You're going to regret your decision by the end of the day. I could have returned home to visit with my brother and be back again before you'd noticed I'd gone."

"I always notice the minute you stepped out the door." Ambrose stepped close and cupped Francis' jaw. "If I complain later, you can scold me like a good wife should."

He scowled. "I'd hope you'd end that particular joke."

The duke kissed him and grinned. "Not a chance. I imagine I could get a good many miles out of it still. What sort of wife shall you be?"

A possessive one. A wife was a permanent feature in a man's life. But Ambrose had avoided all permanent attachments since the duchess had died. Would he give up flirting? It was doubtful, but Francis didn't know how to respond. Some gentlemen *did* marry each other in clandestine ceremonies. None of them could be acknowledged. He shook his head. "You are incorrigible."

"I am happy. Get used to it." His lover closed a hand over Francis' arse and squeezed. "I am determined to be the perfect husband, too. Devoted, faithful, ready and willing to adore."

Francis' heart pounded. "You really mean that, don't you?"

"Of course." Ambrose drew them closer together. "Who else would put up with me? Who else will speak their mind to me as you have always done? We are very well matched, Francis. Better than I imagined, and I have imagined quite a bit. Now, let's get ourselves underway and home to Tindel Park before I get carried away and need to be scolded."

"The carriage *is* ready."

Ambrose kissed him softly. "And it *is* a long drive. But we have plenty of time alone with no interruptions."

He struggled to keep his lust under control, but he was fighting a losing battle. The duke's kisses were taking his caution away. "You should rest during the trip."

The duke swept his tongue inside Francis' mouth, deepening the kiss until all he could think about was pleasure. Francis curled his fingers into the lush brocaded waistcoat before him and jerked their hips closer together. The hard ridge of the duke's erection bumped his.

"You shall be lucky if I don't seduce you before we even get underway," Ambrose whispered. "I saw pillows and blankets being stowed inside the carriage."

"I thought of your comfort."

"Such a good wife to take care of me." The duke's slow grin and slow moving hand forced a groan from his lips. "I've thought of nothing else but touching you. It's going to be a very wicked trip, Francis. Do you still want to leave me behind?"

"No." He swallowed. "I had a night terror, thinking about what you could get up to alone."

"Nowhere near enough mischief with you gone. From now on, we do everything together. Agreed?"

Francis slipped his hand over the duke's erection and stroked. "Agreed."

EPILOGUE

Fishing was a job requiring patience, determination and an unwillingness to admit defeat, which was why Ambrose lay on the river bank getting some sun while his lover did all the fishing. He marveled that Francis was still at it after three hours of intermittent nibbles. He'd given up long ago in favor of reclining half-naked in a sheltered spot that gave him complete privacy.

Perhaps that was the problem.

He hadn't removed enough clothes to attract Francis' attention. He rolled onto his back, slipped the buttons of his trousers undone and lifted his feet up into the air. He tugged off his trousers and smalls. This lying about idly in the sun made him amorous, which is why they came here twice a week. No one came looking for them here in fear of scaring away the fish.

And twice a week they didn't have to muffle their voices from passing servants who didn't have a clue so far that their master was completely and irrevocably in love with Francis Redding. He set his feet to the blanket and stroked his cock.

Terribly in love and Francis had no clue.

Something heavy dropped beside his head. Then Francis crawled over him and pressed a quick kiss to his lips. "I have your supper."

"I have something for you, too."

"That old thing." Francis looked down with a grin. "I've had it before."

"Oh, shut up. Stop reminding me that my birthday just passed."

Francis cupped his balls gently. "So old."

Blood surged to his cock. "Still able to fuck you twice a day. It would be more often if the damn servants would disappear for longer."

"Shh, stop complaining. You'll ruin your day."

"Our day." Ambrose countered. "How is your brother getting along?"

"As bad a patient as you, but he's recovering nicely and shouldn't require my daily visits for too much longer."

"Good." Ambrose pushed his lover onto his side on the blanket and snuggled against him. His heart pounded with anxiety. Could he confess his love here and now? Doing so was fraught with danger. What if Francis didn't love him in return?

He squeezed his eyes shut as Francis wriggled his arse against his cock. Red had taken to being fucked as a duck took to water. He seemed to love the attention and was always willing when Ambrose wanted him. He rarely took the initiative and Ambrose had started to worry that he wasn't enough.

"Ambrose?"

He set a hand to his hip. The heat of his skin burned his fingers and he shuffled until his cock was better positioned. With a small adjustment, he entered a bit without the aid of lubrication.

Francis shuddered. "I love you."

His heart stopped. "You love me?"

Red shook his head violently. "Forget I said that out loud."

"Oh, no, I won't." He wrapped his arms about his lover and crushed him against his chest. "You really love me?"

"No, you idiot. I meant Tindel Park."

Ambrose set his mouth against the hard muscles and nipped the warm skin. "Liar. You said you loved me." His heart raced and he lifted Francis' upper leg and pressed deeper into his body. The tight ring gave grudgingly, eased no doubt by their earlier tryst. When he was deep, he pulled Francis against him and stoked a hand over his rippling stomach.

Francis looked over his shoulder. "Heaven help me, I do."

He smiled as he curled a hand around Francis' heavy cock. He stroked once. "I have a confession too." He stroked again, keeping his touch light and his hips still.

"What have you done now?" Francis grumbled, he shifted his hips in search of more pleasure.

Ambrose laughed against his lover's shoulder. He'd done the unthinkable. He'd fallen in love at the advanced age of five and forty and was smitten with his new life with Francis. This was exactly the best life could offer a man like him. He had everything he wanted and more. "Nothing too drastic. Nor life threatening." He met Francis' puzzled gaze and smiled. "I'm in love with you, too."

THE END

ABOUT THE AUTHOR

Bestselling historical author Heather Boyd believes every character she creates deserves their own happily-ever-after, no matter how much trouble she puts them through. With that goal in mind, she weaves sizzling English set love stories that push the boundaries of regency era propriety to keep readers enthralled until the wee hours of the morning. Brimming with new ideas, she frequently wishes she could type as fast as she conjures new storylines. While writing full time north of Sydney, Australia, Heather collects dust bunnies in all corners of the house and does her best to wrangle her testosterone-fuelled family into submission.

For more information visit
www.heather-boyd.com

ALSO BY HEATHER BOYD

The Distinguished Rogues Series:
Chills
Broken
Charity
An Accidental Affair
Keepsake
An Improper Proposal
Reason to Wed
The Trouble with Love
Married by Moonlight

The Wild Randalls Series:
Engaging the Enemy
Forsaking the Prize
Guarding the Spoils
Hunting the Hero

Miss Mayhem Series:
Miss Watson's First Scandal
Miss George's Second Chance
Miss Radley's Third Dare

Short Stories:
One Wicked Night
Wicked Mourning
In the Widow's Bed
Love Me Tender
Love Me True
The Almack's Alternative
A Husband for Mary

The Hunt Club Series

ALMOST AN EQUAL

When the Duke of Byworth's empty marriage is threatened by a fellow duke he is naturally aggrieved. Nathan cannot allow the potentially damaging contents of his wife's diary to reveal the depths of their estrangement because exposure of his secret dalliances with other men would taint his innocent children's lives. Not to mention end his life. So, without revealing his mission to his steward, Henry Stackpool, a man he trusts for everything else, Nathan undertakes to steal the diary back alone.

Former pickpocket and molly house whore, Henry Stackpool, works hard to keep his position as right hand to a moral man, the Duke of Byworth, but he fears his kind hearted employer is ill-equipped for a confrontation with his unstable opponent. Henry cannot explain the source of his knowledge without exposing the secrets of his past. So when fate places Henry in harm's way, he risks his hard won reputation and freedom to retrieve the duchess's diary himself.

BARELY A MASTER

The trappings of wealth and power give Aiden Banks, Duke of Lewes, little joy and certainly no pleasure. Tormented by grave mistakes he made in the past, he's learned control of his temper at great personal cost, finally shouldering the blame that he has lost the only man he had ever loved through his own actions. His only remaining goal is to educate his young heir to take his place as duke and then he will be free of his responsibilities.

Terrance Bridgewater has freedom at long last with no one to slow down his pursuit of reckless adventure. In London briefly en route to a ship bound for the continent, brings him face to face with his past. Running into the dark and dangerous Duke of Lewes is a complication he'd hoped to avoid. Despite his mistrust, the volatile duke's plea for a second chance tempts Terrance to lower his guard but on his terms only. Yet what can come of two souls with nothing in common but lies, opposing desires, and with far different futures ahead?

On the surface, Raphael has everything he needs: good friends, a title, and membership to the decadent Hunt Club where forbidden pleasure can be had at a moments notice. Pretending is not what he wants. Expectations by family and friends keep his feelings for Lord Claymore at bay. When his best friend returns to London in a black mood, Rafe sets out to cheer him up and make Claymore's upcoming birthday an event to remember.

Shaken and uneasy of his growing attraction to men, James has reached an uncomfortable crossroads in his well-ordered, respectable life. Plans to end his torment on his birthday are mere days away. However, his intention to explore forbidden passion just once comes unstuck. Can James follow through with his well-reasoned, sensible decision when a man who knows what he wants, needs him too?

NEVER A GENTLEMAN

Victor Knight has never been able to juggle his work and love life to anyone's satisfaction. A hardworking investment banker in London, he's obsessed with maintaining his clients' privacy and profits, and cannot understand why those same clients are withdrawing funds when he's making them a good profit. When a dull evening supper at the Hunt Club ends in a blunt invitation to have sex with the Earl of Beecroft, he welcomes the distraction on the proviso they never discuss his business affairs.

Daniel Wellham, the Earl of Beecroft, has long admired Victor Knight. He even understands and admires the banker's preoccupation with work. Their night together is everything he hoped it would be and while he longs for permanence, his secret life as a spy means he can never reveal too much of his own history. Unfortunately, when he realizes that all is not right in Victor's life, those promises he made to keep his nose out of the banker's business means he cannot offer to help or explain that his latest mission might take him away forever. How can love and trust be possible when duty and responsibility prevent total honesty?

www.ingramcontent.com/pod-product-compliance
Lightning Source LLC
Chambersburg PA
CBHW030646190726

48286CB00008B/2688